COME HOME TO THE BRIDE

RETURN TO BLESSING, TEXAS
BOOK SIX

LACEY DAVIS

Three hearts, one love—will they risk it all for a second chance?

Being left at the altar was devastating, but for Regina, it was the final confirmation—she didn't need a man. After all, who needs love when all it brings is heartache? Retreating to her family's lakehouse, she swears off men for good. But her resolve is tested when two very familiar faces show up: Harley Kerr and Jackson Moore, her high school sweethearts—the two men who broke her heart years ago.

Harley and Jackson left Blessing, Texas, to chase adventure in the Navy, leaving Regina behind with nothing but memories of what could've been. Now, six years later, they're back—battle-scarred, ruggedly handsome, and determined to turn their newly purchased ranch into a home. But there's something else they both want: a second chance with the one woman they've never forgotten.

Jackson is done running from his feelings, and Harley knows walking away from Regina was the biggest mistake of his life. With a family feud threatening their ranch, they'll need her strength as much as she needs their love. But can Regina trust the men who once broke her heart? And will she open herself up to a love so powerful it could heal all three of them?

Return to Blessing, Texas

Come Home to the Cowboys
Come Home to the Ranch
Come Home to the Lawmen
Come Home to the Country
Come Home to the Doctor's
Come Home to the Bride
Return to Blessing, Texas Books 1-3
Return to Blessing, Texas Books 4-6

Want to learn about my new releases before anyone else?
Sign up for my https://laceydavisauthor.com/mailing-list
and receive a complimentary book.

CHAPTER 1

It was my wedding day, and I, Regina Nash, was supposed to marry Edward Bartholomew III.

We'd known each other since college and had been friends long before romance entered the picture. And while I knew Ed loved me, his family was a different story. They'd never approved of me or my family's "lifestyle"—and by that, they meant my two fathers. I loved both my dads equally, and our family wasn't even unusual where I was from.

In Blessing, plenty of families were like ours. Even my brothers had followed the family tradition of sharing a wife with another man.

But Ed's mother was a prude, and his father had always looked at me like I was some kind of gold digger. His parents had their own narrow ideas, and despite my love for him, a small part of me couldn't shake the worry that their influence might someday come between us.

"Are you ready, love?" My mother's voice cut through my thoughts, soft and steady.

I looked at her, took a deep breath, and nodded. "Yes."

One of my dads, Mack, stood by, his expression serious. "Are you sure, honey? This is your last chance to back out if you're having any doubts. We want you to be happy."

"Daddy, I'm sure," I said with a smile, hoping I sounded more certain than I felt. "Ed loves me, and I love him. We'll work through any issues with his family."

My second dad, Tim, stepped forward, taking my hand. "If there's any doubt, now's the time to call it off. His family will never accept us, and that's okay. But I want you to be certain."

"No doubts," I replied, squeezing his hand. "Well, maybe one—that I can't have you both walk me down the aisle." Ed's family wouldn't budge on that, so I'd had to choose one of my dads. The sting of that compromise lingered.

"All right, let's get this wedding started," my mother said with a smile, though her eyes held a touch of worry.

After another round of hugs, my parents left the room, leaving me with one final thought: if Ed's family couldn't even handle the idea of both my fathers giving me away, how would they cope with my life or my values? I pushed the thought aside. We'd figure it out. As long as we had love, we'd be fine.

The music began, and I took one last look at myself in the mirror before heading to the church door with my dad. We moved into the vestibule where the wedding party had gathered, and I heard a hum of murmurs through the closed doors of the chapel. Something felt off. The usual excitement of a wedding crowd wasn't there.

The doors opened, and I watched my mother rush down the aisle toward the groom's quarters. I turned to follow her, the uneasy feeling twisting tighter. By the time I reached the room, she was staring at an envelope on a table, her expression ashen.

"What's going on?" I asked, my voice cracking, not seeing Edward in the room.

"Give this to Regina," one of Ed's groomsmen muttered, practically shoving the envelope into my mother's hands. His face was frozen in shock, and when she handed it to me, her fingers trembled.

I ripped open the envelope, and as I read Ed's letter, everything shattered.

Regina,

I'm sorry. I can't marry you. My family won't accept your family, and if I marry you, they'll disinherit me. Please don't try to find me; I've left the country.

Ed

A bitter laugh forced its way up, and before I knew it, I was laughing hysterically, tears streaming down my face as the humiliation set in. My parents rushed to my side, holding me as I crumpled against them.

"It's okay, sweetheart," my dad murmured. "He didn't deserve you."

"What kind of person waits until the last minute to do this?" my mother snapped, her voice thick with anger and tears. "I'll kill him if I ever see him again."

Ed's family hadn't liked me. They hadn't even liked that he was marrying a girl from Blessing, a town that embraced love in all its forms. And if Ed couldn't stand up to them for me before the wedding, I knew he'd never stand up for me afterward. Still, he could've spared me this public humiliation.

Why hadn't he called me? Told me? Instead, he'd let me prepare like nothing was wrong while he slipped away on their private jet. Asshole.

"Get me out of here," I whispered. "And get me out of this dress."

My mother held my arm as we made our way back to the dressing room. My sisters-in-law, my bridesmaids, helped me slip out of the wedding gown, careful not to rip the delicate fabric. I pulled on the jeans I'd packed for our honeymoon, numbness creeping in as I heard the low buzz of people filing out of the church, whispering about the spectacle of a bride left at the altar.

"I'm going to the cabin," I said, steadying my voice. I didn't want to stay in Blessing where everyone's sympathetic stares would follow me.

My mother's face fell. "No, honey. You don't need to be alone right now. You need family around you."

I shook my head. "What I need is space. I need fresh air and quiet. I promise I'll be fine. I just need some time."

My father gave my mother a look, then nodded. "All right, but you check in once a day, or I'll be up there to bring you back myself."

"Thank you," I said, hugging them tightly. "I'll be fine. I'll spend the month up there, rest, and write that scathing novel I've always wanted to write about a bride left at the altar."

A faint smile crossed my mother's face. "Things happen for a reason. He didn't deserve you. And next time, you'll find someone who does."

I didn't have the heart to tell her that "next time" felt impossibly far away. The man I'd thought would stand by me had chosen money over love. And the irony? I had a trust fund that made his family's wealth look like pocket change.

No, I didn't tell him about it because I wanted to wait until after we were married. His mistake.

The drive up to the cabin was quiet, the winding mountain roads offering a kind of balm that I desperately needed. When I arrived, I didn't bother unpacking. I simply stood at the edge of the mountain creek, letting the brisk wind and the sound of water soothe the ache inside me. Here, I could be alone. I could heal.

And once I blocked Ed's number and deleted his texts, I would be able to do just that. There would be no second chance, no groveling apology that could win me back. The peace and beauty of the mountains stretched in front of me, promising me what I needed most: freedom from everything he had taken from me. Freedom to heal.

CHAPTER 2

I stared at the framed law degree above my attorney Nathan Alley's desk and let out a long, frustrated sigh. I never imagined fighting for my birthright, especially against family.

"My parents left me that ranch," I said, forcing down my irritation. "They wanted it in my hands. Serving in the Navy shouldn't have changed that."

Nathan nodded, his eyes sympathetic but pragmatic. "I know, Jackson, and legally, you're in the right. But while you were serving, your uncle took over. Now he's claiming the property should rightfully be his. We'll likely need to start with an eviction notice and, depending on his response, might end up in court."

I shook my head, running a hand over my face. "I asked him to look after it. Just to keep an eye on the place until I got back. Now he's got his herd on my land, changed the locks on the gates, and moved into the house. It's like he's made himself right at home."

Nathan leaned back. "First things first. We'll serve the

eviction notice, and then we'll work on removing his cattle. Either he clears out his herd, or we send him an invoice for grazing on your land."

I stood, feeling both grateful and weary. "Thanks, Nathan. Let me know what you find out. I've tried calling my uncle, but after the first conversation where he told me not to think about coming home, he stopped picking up."

That call still stung. Family was supposed to be there for you, especially when you were halfway around the world in uniform. Instead, I came back to find my uncle squatting on my land, acting like he was doing me a favor.

Nathan rose and walked me to the door. "I'll keep you posted, Jackson. And, hey, congratulations on making it back to Blessing. I'm glad you're finally home."

"Excuse my manners," Jackson said, "but congratulations on the birth of your son and marrying Lillian. I'm happy for you." The man had what he wanted – a wife and family.

After spending his time in the Navy, I had come home hoping to find what I wanted.

The only problem was she'd gotten married this weekend.

"Thank you. I feel so blessed," Nathan said, grinning. "It was a struggle not too far from what you're going through, but in the end, Lillian and Colt finally reached an agreement on the land. I hope we can get you a satisfying conclusion as well."

"Thanks," I said, stepping outside and taking a deep breath. The small town stretched out in front of me, so familiar, yet changed. I'd dreamed of this place through all those years in the Navy, of coming back here, running the ranch, building a life of my own. I wasn't about to let that dream slip away, even if it meant showing my uncle the door myself.

My mother had always told me that her brother was ruthless, and now I believed her. Carlos Thomas White was just a chip off the block from his father, my grandfather Daniel White. Mom had always said to not trust either man. She'd been right.

When you were out of town serving the military, you didn't have many options for someone to look out for the ranch. My uncle had volunteered, and I reluctantly agreed.

Now, I regretted that decision.

"Get in the truck," Harley said, his voice urgent. Lost in thought, I didn't see him coming up behind me.

We had been best friends since the second grade and had even gone into the Navy together.

"What's going on? I thought we'd grab lunch, maybe head out to the ranch and try talking to my uncle together."

Harley shook his head, his eyes intense. "Regina's groom backed out of the wedding."

My heart kicked hard in my chest. "What?"

"We need to go see her," he said, already sliding into the passenger seat.

I jumped in beside him, my pulse pounding. "What kind of idiot leaves a woman like Regina at the altar?"

Harley snorted, anger sparking in his eyes. "Apparently, the groom's parents didn't like our town's, uh, traditions. They didn't approve of Regina's family or her having two dads, and they were scared she'd convince their son to have another man in their marriage."

He was right; our town of Blessing had unique customs that outsiders rarely understood. When Blessing was first settled, there were more men than women, and rather than fight over wives, they'd decided to share. It had become tradition—one man took the legal title of husband while the other was an equal partner in every other way. Blessing was built on that tradition, and most families here carried it on. Regina's family was no exception.

I gripped the steering wheel as I drove. "Back in school, Regina was so angry with us when we told her we had enlisted in the Navy."

"And then she broke up with us," Harley added. "She didn't want to sit around waiting."

I clenched my jaw, feeling the old frustration. "She was eighteen and wanted freedom. I get it. But are we over her?"

Harley looked out the window, shoulders tense. "We met plenty of women in the Navy, and none of them could hold a candle to her. I still dream about her. About… about all of us being together. I thought I'd be over it by now, but here I am."

I laughed, shaking my head. "That's why you came running up to me, telling me we have to go see her?"

He cracked a smile. "I don't know. It felt like fate telling me she's free, and we need to get to her before anyone else steps in."

When we pulled up to Regina's family ranch, memories hit me hard. This place had been like a second home. Her parents had welcomed us in as kids, treating us like family. Even after all these years, it felt like coming home.

As we climbed out of the truck, I shot Harley a look. "What are we even going to say? 'Sorry your wedding fell apart; would you consider us instead?'"

Harley laughed, a mix of humor and tension. "Hell, if I know. I just want to see her. See if that connection's still there. Show her that we're still here and still care."

I nodded, taking a steadying breath as we walked up to the front door. Harley rang the bell, and a moment later, Mack Nash, Regina's dad, opened the door.

"Boys! Good to see you." He pulled us inside, clapping us

on the shoulders. "I heard you're back in town. How was the Navy?"

"It was the Navy," Harley said, shaking his head. "Lots of rules and regulations."

"Heard you boys are Navy SEALs," Mack said, admiration in his voice.

"Yeah," I replied, memories of grueling training flashing through my mind. "It was tough, but we made it through."

"Is Regina here," Harley asked.

"Come on in, we'll talk," Mack said, leading us to the living room. "Regina's mom and Tim are here too. Tim, look who's here!"

Tim walked in, followed by Mrs. Nash. Her face lit up, and she came over, pulling us both into a warm hug. "My boys! It's so good to see you back safe."

Tim shook our hands. "Glad to see you survived the military."

"Us too," I said, exchanging a look with Harley.

Mack chuckled, looking at us with a twinkle in his eye. "So, you boys were asking about Regina?"

We both nodded, glancing at each other. Harley spoke first. "Yeah, is she here?"

Tim exchanged a look with his wife. "Did you hear what happened at the wedding?"

"No," Harley said, glancing at me, his expression a mix of hope and something like anticipation.

Mrs. Nash's face tightened. "The groom's parents convinced him to back out. They thought we weren't good enough for them, and they didn't want Regina bringing another man into the marriage. The coward didn't even tell her himself; he left a note with his groomsmen. If I ever see that boy again…"

I felt a rush of anger for Regina, knowing all the plans she must have made and what she'd gone through.

"Where is she now?" I asked.

"She's up at the mountain cabin," Tim said. "Wanted some space to clear her head, work on her novel, do some fly-fishing. We told her to check in with us every day, or we'd come up to get her."

Harley's face lit up. "So she's alone?"

Mrs. Nash nodded, a small smile playing on her lips. "She's all alone. You boys were always close to her. I'd always dreamed you two would be her husbands."

So had I. But Regina had gone to college, and we'd gone to the Navy. She hadn't wanted to wait, and we hadn't expected her to. But that didn't make the sting any less.

"Why'd you break up?" Mack asked, his gaze sharp.

Harley shrugged, glancing at me. "We were leaving, and she wanted freedom."

Tim leaned back, grinning. "Well, you're back now. You're free."

We were. But did she still want us? There was only one way to find out.

"With your permission," I said, "we'd like to go up there, talk to her. See if…" I trailed off, not entirely sure what I was asking for.

Mack looked at Tim, then his wife, before nodding. "Regina's in a fragile state, boys. She's been hurt. I'm not against you going up there, but if you hurt my girl…"

Tim gave us a stern nod. "You've always been our choice for her. Whoever marries her will be one lucky man."

Mrs. Nash laughed softly. "Boys, I'm thrilled you're going up there. That way, she won't be alone. And you have my blessing. I won't tell her you're coming; she'll say she doesn't want to see anyone. But you two showing up on her doorstep will be the best surprise she's had in weeks."

"Yes, ma'am," Harley said, standing. "We'll leave at first light."

Mack clapped me on the shoulder as we turned to leave. "And Jackson, if you need help with your uncle, let me know. That son of a bitch is a parasite."

"Thanks, sir," I said, shaking his hand. "Right now, I'm letting Nathan Alley handle the eviction, but if it comes to it, I'll do what's needed."

I turned and gave Mrs. Nash a hug, whispering, "We'll take care of her. Don't worry."

"I know you will, son," she replied with a knowing smile.

In that moment, I felt ready for whatever lay ahead, my mind set. Tomorrow, we'd find out if fate was still on our side.

CHAPTER 3

Three days. It had been three days since Ed left me standing at the altar, and I still felt hollow, like the last three years had been yanked out from under me. I didn't know if he'd tried to contact me because I'd blocked him. There would be no second chances, no reunion, no apology that could fix this. We were done. Stick a fork in him, as far as I was concerned.

He should have been man enough to tell me he was wavering. To tell me face-to-face or even just pick up the phone. But instead, he'd slithered out in the morning light, leaving me standing there, dressed in my wedding gown, with our family and friends all packed into the church. The shock on their faces still burned in my memory. And the humiliation? That wasn't going anywhere anytime soon.

To make things worse, I'd found out his family had given him an ultimatum: marry me and he'd be out of the family estate. Like I was some filthy secret he had to hide. I should've known when they looked down their noses at my family for

"

having two dads. To them, that was a scandalous arrangement, a moral flaw I apparently inherited by association.

I took a deep breath and cast my line out across the clear water. The rhythmic pull of the fly rod, the rushing stream, the fresh mountain air—those were my peace now. The cabin had been a godsend, a safe haven far from everyone who had an opinion on my "tragedy" or thought they knew what was best for me. Just a few days of solitude and fly-fishing on the family property here in Colorado, and I'd already begun to feel the knots in my chest loosen.

The place itself was more than just a cabin. It was a four-bedroom, three-bath mountain home with everything I needed, including a kitchen I actually loved cooking in. I wake up early, step out onto the deck with my coffee, and watch deer nibble on the trees or drink from the creek. Last night, I'd even chased off a curious raccoon who'd decided to raid the trash bins. Peace, nature, and quiet were good medicine.

A sharp tug on the line jolted me back, and I reeled in a nice-sized rainbow trout. "Supper," I said aloud, admiring the fish before slipping it into my pouch. I figured one or two more would do, enough to last a few meals since I wasn't keen on cooking for just myself. I hated those prepackaged meals but I got some at the store and shoved them into the freezer along with some steak, but fresh trout sounded like the best comfort food.

I cast again, letting the gentle babble of the stream soothe my mind. I knew my family was worried about me, but I just needed time. Just a few days to breathe and sort out what came next.

The thought of going back to Austin was a non-starter. Ed and I had shared a tiny rental for six months while planning the wedding. I'd already moved my things out and had canceled the down payment on the house we were supposed to close on right after the honeymoon. I'd heard he went off to the Caribbean with his parents, our supposed honeymoon turning into a family vacation.

A sigh slipped out as I flicked the line again, letting the fly skim the surface of the water. Just then, another tug—another trout on the line. As I reeled it in, I heard the low rumble of thunder rolling over the mountains. Afternoon showers were part of life up here, but that meant I'd need to pack up soon. In these parts, it only took a few minutes for flash floods to race down the mountainside, and I wasn't planning on getting caught in one.

I glanced over my shoulder at the sound of an engine, squinting at the classy pickup truck lumbering up the dirt road to the cabin. Hopefully, just a lost hiker or someone needing directions. But as I removed the second trout from my line, the doors of the truck slammed shut, and I heard my name.

"Regina!" The voice hit me with the force of a memory—familiar, strong, and, damn it, alluring. I knew that voice. Loved that man at one time.

Turning around, I found myself face to face with Jackson and Harley, the two men I'd given my heart to back in high school. The two I'd never really forgotten, no matter how much time or distance were between us. What in the world were they doing here?

Jackson stepped forward, quiet confidence in his gaze, and Harley followed, all muscles and ruggedness with the same boyish smile I remembered. They both looked like they'd just walked off some recruitment poster, tall and lean, their jeans fitting in all the right ways. Though they wore cowboy hats, I could tell by their short haircuts they hadn't long left the military. Last I'd heard, they were Navy SEALs.

"What are you doing here?" I said, after reeling in my line and walking toward them, heart pounding.

Harley's smile was crooked, that damn charming smile that still hit me straight in the gut. "We wanted to see you."

My mind raced, searching for reasons, and one thought came to the surface: my mother. I could practically feel her hand in this, sending them here to "rescue" me. The last thing I needed right now was a blast from the past, two men who'd left for the Navy while I went off to college, and I tried to put them behind me.

"I thought you were in the Navy," I said, avoiding the question.

Jackson nodded, his voice steady as always. "We were. Just got back to Blessing a couple days ago."

Just in time to hear about my disaster of a wedding, no doubt.

"What are you doing here?" I repeated, folding my arms, trying to keep my distance in more ways than one.

They exchanged a look, and Harley spoke first. "We came to see you. To clear up some old business."

I let out a mirthless laugh. "Well, I'm not interested in clearing up any business, old or new. Not right now. I'm officially over men."

That got a grin out of both of them.

"Well, we're not over you," Jackson said softly, his eyes holding mine.

My heart gave a traitorous leap, and I felt the stirrings of something I hadn't let myself feel in a long time. Not for them.

"Look, I came here to write, to decompress. Being left at the altar? Not exactly a breeze to get over."

Jackson took another step toward me, and before I knew what was happening, he'd pulled me into his arms. My instinct was to resist, to pull back, but the warmth of his body and the familiar, woodsy scent of him melted my defenses. In that moment, being held, feeling those strong arms around me… it felt like something clicked back into place.

It felt like I traveled back to high school and how we'd like to go to the park and push our bodies to the limits without actual penetration. We'd never made love, but we'd come damn close. And at that time, I'd been so confused. I wanted Harley and Jackson, but I wasn't certain I wanted two husbands. Now, I didn't know what I wanted.

"I'm sorry, Regina," he whispered, his voice low. "Just say the word, and I'll find him and kick his ass for you."

A soft laugh escaped me as I eased back. "No need to go to jail for me, Jackson. Thanks, though." I glanced from him to Harley, who watched us with that familiar twinkle in his green eyes. "Look, I appreciate the gesture, but I came here for time alone."

A loud crack of thunder echoed off the mountains, making the decision for us. I glanced at the sky, knowing that at any moment, rain would start falling.

Harley stepped forward, boots crunching on gravel. "Let us stay for supper. We'll clean the fish, you fry them, and then we'll leave. You can tell us about the writing, the fishing, whatever you want to talk about."

He had a way of saying things like it was the most natural idea in the world, even if the suggestion made my pulse race. But cleaning fish was my least favorite chore, and I hated the smell that seemed to linger no matter what I did. Sending them back down the mountain now felt almost cruel, especially when they'd driven all the way from Texas.

I bit my lip, mulling it over. "Fine," I said finally. "You clean the fish, and I'll cook them up." I handed Harley the fish bag, trying to keep my face neutral, but his grin was impossible to ignore.

"Deal," he said, sharing a triumphant glance with Jackson. He looked every bit as handsome as I remembered with those green eyes that could probably convince anyone to do just about anything.

Jackson chuckled, nudging him. "You volunteered, so you're cleaning them. I'll help Regina up to the house and, if she doesn't mind, help her remove those waders."

I rolled my eyes but couldn't help the little smile tugging at my lips. "Don't get too excited, Jackson. I've got yoga pants on underneath."

Thunder rumbled, and the rain began to fall softly. Memories of late-night bonfires, sneaking out to the lake, and their warm hands in mine crept up on me. We'd been close once, so close that I'd thought of a future with them until they'd left. I'd let them go, convinced we were all too young and that they'd forget me as soon as they were gone.

But now, standing there with them, the past felt closer than ever.

As Harley walked toward the back of the house, Jackson offered his arm with a grin. "After you, Miss Nash. Let's get you out of those waders and into the kitchen."

I shook my head, knowing I'd already lost this battle. "All right," I said, smiling despite myself. "But if you're staying, you're peeling the potatoes."

CHAPTER 4

I finished cleaning the trout, and as I walked toward the cabin, I felt a pull in my chest. The rain clouds were thickening, and thunder rumbled closer, echoing in the mountains. A cold breeze swept over the yard, carrying the promise of rain. The smell of wet pine and earth filled the air. This cabin felt like home more than anything had in years.

Inside, I found Regina and Jackson working in sync, and it almost made me smile. Regina tossed a salad, her movements smooth and practiced while Jackson wrestled with a peeler, struggling with a pile of potatoes.

"Looks like she put you to work," I said, trying to keep the amusement out of my voice.

Jackson raised an eyebrow, smirking as he handed a peeled potato to Regina. "Yeah, lucky you got the manly job," he muttered.

Regina chuckled. "You're welcome to make the salad, Jackson."

He held up his hands in surrender. "No thanks. I'll stick with the potatoes."

Her gaze softened when she turned to me, something warm in her eyes. "Put those fish in the sink, Harley. Once Jackson's got the potatoes frying, I'll get started on them."

I nodded, taking in the sight of her, the way she fit so naturally into this place. "Got any whiskey around here?" I asked, half-joking. I already knew it wouldn't help the dull ache in my head, the one that had been creeping in since we got here.

My body no longer adjusted to altitude and temperature changes the way it once had. In fact, the military had left my body in a ragged state. One I didn't know if I would ever fully recover from.

She shook her head, firm. "Not tonight. You're still adjusting to the altitude. Last thing we need is you driving off the side of the mountain because you couldn't handle your liquor."

"All right," I said, raising my hands. It was hard to argue when she looked out for me like that, even after all these years. "What can I do to help?"

She glanced around and smiled. "Set the table, maybe. We'd eat on the deck, but..." She trailed off as thunder cracked overhead, and the rain came down, rattling the windows and casting a cozy hush over the room.

With the rain, the temperature had dropped and I couldn't help but think it would be a great night for a fire.

Jackson glanced outside, his face serious. "Wow, it's really coming down."

"It usually passes fast," Regina said with a shrug, handing him an onion. "Dice this with the potatoes."

Jackson sighed, looking at me as if to say, *rescue me.*

"I had to clean fish; you can handle an onion," I said with a grin.

He grumbled but got to chopping. I watched them for a moment, the three of us moving in this easy, familiar rhythm. I'd missed this. Years ago, we had been inseparable except for the nights.

As Regina seasoned the fish and coated it in cornmeal, I busied myself setting the table, the memories of times past flooding back. It felt surreal being here again, doing this again. But then, as I bent over to straighten a plate, my vision blurred, and the familiar pulse of pain started up at the base of my skull.

I braced myself against the table, reaching into my pocket for aspirin and swallowing them dry. Too many hits, too many close calls, and the headaches were my constant companion.

And if I wasn't going to survive these headaches, I wanted a son or daughter to inherit what I had built. No, it wasn't much, but I wanted someone with my genes and DNA to be walking this earth. Therefore, I wanted a wife. Someone to love.

"Everything's ready; let's eat!" Regina's voice cut through the haze, pulling me back to the present.

Jackson glanced at her, frowning. "I thought you said the rain would pass quickly?"

She gave him a wry smile, looking out the window. "Normally, it does." She squinted, then cursed softly. "The creek's out of its banks. Jackson, you'd better move your truck up closer to the house before it goes swimming downstream."

I gave him a quick shake of my head as he glanced my way, silently letting him know I wasn't up for braving the rain. He nodded, stepping out into the storm without another word. When he came back in, his hair and shirt were soaked.

Regina glanced at Jackson. "It's still coming down."

"Yes," he said pulling the wet shirt off. Underneath, he wore a T-shirt that clung to his muscles. One thing every Navy SEAL had in common was the muscles we acquired. And Jackson had a well-defined six pack.

We gathered around the table. It felt almost too good, sitting there with them like we'd stepped back in time. As we ate, Jackson broke the quiet, looking at Regina.

"Did you love Ed?"

Her fork paused mid-air, her eyes darkening. "I thought I did," she said finally, her voice low. "But his family never accepted me. They couldn't see past the fact that I have two dads." She glanced down at her plate. "Now, I don't know. I'm disappointed that his parents could convince him not to marry me. To leave me standing there at the altar."

I knew all too well how people could be. "It's funny how people get hung up on things like that," I said, feeling the weight of my family history. My family was rock-solid until one of my dads died. After that, everything changed.

I never thought my remaining two parents would divorce, but they had. And my mother had moved away.

Jackson gave a slow nod, his eyes soft with sympathy. "My father passed three years ago, and then Mom got cancer. Lost her six months back."

Regina's gaze softened as she reached across the table, resting a hand on his. "I'm so sorry, Jackson. I always loved your parents."

"Yeah, me too." He sighed, staring down at his plate. "For years, I thought about your family, Regina, and wished mine was more like yours."

She smiled, a sad sort of smile that cut right to the heart. "They are the best." She turned her gaze on me, her expression thoughtful. "You look better now, Harley."

I managed a small smile, the warmth of the food and the closeness easing the ache in my head. "It's good to be here," I said.

A comfortable silence settled over us, the sound of the rain, the warmth of the fire, the food, and comfortable conversation filling the space between us. For the first time in years, I felt like I could breathe easy.

Then Jackson, as he often did, stirred the damn pot. The man just couldn't seem to accept peace. He was always looking for answers.

"Regina, why didn't you wait for us?"

The question hung heavy, and I felt the tension tighten in my gut as she set her fork down, eyes narrowing. "You want to get into that?" I asked.

She took a deep breath, staring down at the table. "Look, I was eighteen. I didn't know if you'd ever come back, either of you. You went off to play soldier, and I went to college to live my life. I wasn't going to sit around waiting. And I didn't want you waiting for me either."

Before I could stop myself, the words tumbled out. "Do you still wonder what it would've been like, the three of us?"

Her gaze flicked to me, her voice low and uncertain. "I'm questioning everything right now, Harley. I don't know if happily-ever-afters even exist."

The vulnerability in her voice cut deeper than I expected. She got up, taking her plate into the kitchen, and the ache in my chest grew sharper. I followed her, bringing my plate, and stood there, just inches away.

"Regina, I wondered why you broke it off for years." She looked at me, her face open, her eyes searching mine.

"Wait a minute. You guys broke it off with me. You were going to see the world. I wanted to talk marriage, and you had plans for your big adventure that didn't include me. Fine, I decided that I needed adventure as well."

"We didn't break it off," Jackson said his voice rising.

"Yes, you did," she responded.

This was crazy. She thought we wanted to end our relationship with her? That was nuts.

"In my heart, I thought you ended it. And all these years, there has been a place in my heart that still aches for you. It's yours, even if you're not ready to claim it. I didn't want our relationship to end just because we were in the Navy."

"And just how would we have made that work?"

"I don't know," Jackson said.

She held my gaze, her eyes shining with unshed tears, and then, as if it was the most natural thing in the world, she stepped forward, her arms slipping around me. I pulled her close, holding her like I might never get the chance again.

The warmth of her against me, her body fitting against mine, stirred something raw, something I hadn't felt in a long time. I felt her breathe against me, her voice soft and unsteady. "Harley... there's something I need. I need you to make love to me. Wipe away the memories of Ed. Show me what I couldn't see before. Help me to understand if there truly still is anything between us, because we were good together."

The words struck me like lightning. I leaned back, searching her face, needing to be sure. "Are you certain?"

"Yes," she whispered, her hand rising to my cheek, her

thumb brushing gently. "I want both of you. Show me what we could've had."

From the corner of my eye, I saw Jackson standing in the doorway, watching us. He met my gaze, a small smile tugging at his lips.

"With pleasure," he said quietly, stepping forward.

I leaned down, my voice a promise against her ear. "You're ours tonight."

CHAPTER 5

The rain pounded against the cabin, a relentless rhythm that seemed to echo the suddenly frantic pace of my heart. I led Harley and Jackson upstairs, my steps faltering slightly as a mix of anticipation and nervousness surged through me. I hadn't planned this, hadn't expected to find myself in this situation again after so many years, but now that I was here, it felt inevitable.

The bedroom was dimly lit, the only light filtering in from the large windows that looked out over the mountains and the occasional flash of lightning. I turned to face them, my breath catching in my throat as I took in the sight of Harley and Jackson standing side by side. They were both so different, yet so familiar. Harley, with his rugged features and intense gaze, and Jackson, with his boyish charm and warm smile.

Harley stepped forward first, his hands cupping my face gently. His thumb brushed against my cheek, and I leaned into his touch, my eyes fluttering closed. His lips met mine, a soft, slow kiss that deepened as I parted my lips, inviting him in.

His tongue explored my mouth, teasing and tasting, and a shiver ran down my spine.

Jackson moved behind me, his hands resting lightly on my hips. He pressed a kiss to the curve of my neck, his lips warm and soft against my skin. I gasped into Harley's mouth, my body arching back against Jackson as his hands slid up my sides, his thumbs brushing against the underside of my breasts.

Harley broke the kiss, his breath ragged as he rested his forehead against mine. "Are you sure about this, Regina?" he murmured, his voice low and rough.

I nodded, my voice barely a whisper. "Yes. I want this. I want both of you. We've waited years, and it seems fate has brought us together again."

Harley's eyes darkened with desire, and he stepped back, his hands moving to the hem of his shirt. He pulled it off in one swift motion, revealing the hard planes of his chest and the jagged scar that ran down his side. I reached out, my fingers tracing the line of the scar, feeling the ridges and dips beneath my touch.

Jackson's hands moved to the buttons of my shirt, undoing them one by one until the fabric fell open, revealing my lace-covered breasts. He slid the shirt off my shoulders, his fingers trailing down my arms, leaving a path of goose bumps in their wake. He unhooked my bra, his hands cupping my breasts as the lace fell away. I gasped as his thumbs brushed against my nipples, the sensation sending a jolt of pleasure through me.

Harley's hands moved to my yoga pants and slid them down my legs. He knelt before me, his hands trailing up my thighs as he pressed a kiss to the sensitive skin just above my knee. I steadied myself, my hands resting on his shoulders as he hooked his fingers in the waistband of my panties and slid them down.

I stepped out of them, standing naked between the two men. I felt exposed and vulnerable but also powerful and desired.

It was all I could do not to move. I wanted to prance in front of them, to tease them, but more than that, I wanted to feel them deep inside me.

Harley looked up at me, his eyes filled with hunger and need. He leaned in, his breath warm against my skin as he pressed a kiss to the inside of my thigh. I gasped, my hands tightening on his shoulders as his tongue traced a path upward, closer and closer to my center.

Gripping his shoulders, I clung to Harley, my breathing short and shallow, desire making me tremble. How many years had I dreamed of being taken by these two men?

Jackson's hands were still on my breasts, his fingers teasing my nipples, sending waves of pleasure coursing through me. I leaned back against him, my head resting on his shoulder as Harley's mouth found my core. His tongue was hot and insistent, teasing and tasting, driving me wild with desire.

I moaned, my hips bucking against Harley's mouth as Jackson's hands explored my body. He trailed kisses down my neck, his teeth scraping gently against my skin as he nipped at the sensitive spot where my neck met my shoulder. His erection pressed against my back, a hard, insistent reminder of his desire.

Harley's fingers joined his tongue, sliding inside me, stretching and filling me. I cried out, my body writhing as the pleasure built, threatening to consume me. I was close, so close, but I didn't want to come like this. I wanted to feel them inside me, to be connected to them in the most intimate way possible.

"Harley, Jackson," I gasped, my voice barely recognizable. "I need you. Both of you."

"Not tonight," Jackson gasped. "We must prepare you to take us both at the same time. We'll get started tonight. But soon, darling, soon."

Disappointment filled me. I wanted to experience it all with these two men. I wanted the three of us together at once.

Harley looked up at me, his emerald eyes dark with desire. He stood, his hands moving to his own jeans, unbuttoning them and sliding them down his legs. His erection sprang free, hard and ready, and I reached out, my hand wrapping around him. He groaned, his hips thrusting into my touch as I stroked him, feeling the velvety softness of his skin beneath my fingers.

Jackson moved away from me, shedding his clothes quickly. I turned to face him, my hand still on Harley, stroking him as I took in the sight of Jackson's naked body. He was lean and muscled, his skin bronzed from years of working outside. His erection jutted out proudly, a bead of moisture glistening at the tip.

I reached out my other hand to wrap around him, stroking him in time with my movements on Harley. They both groaned, their hips thrusting into my touch as I explored their bodies. I could feel the tension building in them, their muscles tightening as they struggled to maintain control.

"Regina," Harley growled, his hand covering mine, stilling my movements. "You're playing with fire."

I smiled, my voice a low purr. Who was this woman they'd created? I'd never acted this way before. "Maybe I want to get burned. Make me so hot that I'm fire on the inside instead of ice."

Jackson chuckled, his hand sliding down my back, cupping my ass, and then giving it a little slap, which sent tremors through me.

"Oh, you will," he promised. "But not yet."

He scooped me up into his arms, carrying me to the bed and laying me down gently. I scooted back, making room for them as they joined me, one on either side. Harley leaned over me, his lips finding mine in a deep, passionate kiss. I could taste myself on his lips, a heady, intoxicating sensation that only served to fuel my desire.

Jackson's hands were on my body, exploring every curve, every dip. His fingers slid between my legs, finding my core, slick and ready. He slid one finger inside me, then another, stretching and filling me. I moaned into Harley's mouth, my hips bucking against Jackson's hand as he began to move, his fingers sliding in and out of me in a steady rhythm.

Harley broke the kiss, his breath ragged as he looked down at me. "Are you ready, Regina?" he murmured, his voice low and rough.

I nodded, my body aching with need. "Yes, please. I'm ready."

Harley rolled onto his back, pulling me with him so I straddled his hips. His erection pressed against my core, and I rubbed against him, teasing us both. He groaned, his hands gripping my hips, guiding me as I slid down onto him, taking him deep inside me.

I cried out, my body stretching to accommodate him. He filled me completely, his hardness hitting every sensitive spot inside me. I moved slowly at first, then faster, my hips rising and falling as I rode him.

Jackson moved behind me, his hands caressing my back, my hips, my ass. His fingers slid between my cheeks, finding the tight ring of muscle hidden there. I gasped, my body tensing slightly as he began to explore, his finger circling, pressing gently.

"Relax, Regina," he murmured, his voice soft and soothing. "Let me in. Tonight is just about preparing you. Exploring you."

I took a deep breath, forcing my body to relax as Jackson's finger slid inside me. The sensation was strange and foreign but not unpleasant. I began to move again, riding Harley as Jackson's finger moved in time with my movements. The pleasure built, intensifying as the two men filled me, their bodies moving in sync with mine.

Jackson's finger slipped out, replaced by the gentle press of his body along mine. I tensed briefly, not from fear but from the anticipation of the intimacy we were about to share. He feathered soft kisses across my shoulder blades, his hands tracing soothing patterns on my hips. "It's okay, Regina," he whispered. "We've got you."

I took a deep breath, letting my body relax into their embrace. This was Jackson, my past, seeking to join me in the most intimate way possible. Behind me, his breath hitched, his body trembling with the effort of holding back. With his fingers back deep inside me, I wanted more.

"Jackson, fuck me," I cried.

"Not yet, darling, but soon," he whispered. "But I'm going to get my turn at your pussy."

Harley's gaze locked onto mine. His hand reached out, cupping my cheek, his thumb brushing away a tear I hadn't realized had fallen. This was Harley, the strong, steady beat of my heart, anchoring me as I begged Jackson to take me the same way.

"That's it," Jackson whispered in my ear. And then I felt the palm of his hand hit my ass.

Smack.

"Jackson," I gasped. "Please."

Another smack and fire trickled between my butt and my pussy.

"Please," I said again, wanting him deep within me.

"Come for us," he whispered.

They moved with me, their bodies synchronized with mine. We found our rhythm, a dance of give and take, push and pull. The pleasure built, intensifying with each thrust, each touch, each whispered word of longing. I was close, so close, the wave of pleasure threatening to consume me.

"Come for us," he whispered.

Harley leaned forward, his forehead touching mine, his breath mingling with my own. "Let go, Regina," he murmured. "We've got you. We'll always have you."

And with those words, I let go, surrendering to the pleasure, to erasing the memories of my mind and replacing them with the promise of tomorrow.

I cried out, my body convulsing as the orgasm hit, waves of pleasure crashing over me. I felt Harley and Jackson following me over the edge, their bodies tensing as they found their own release. We collapsed into a tangle of limbs, our bodies slick with sweat, our breaths coming in ragged gasps.

For a moment, there was only the sound of the rain against the window and the distant rumble of thunder. Then Harley's arms wrapped around me, pulling me close, his lips pressing a soft kiss to my forehead. "That was... incredible," he murmured.

Jackson echoed the sentiment, his hand reaching out to stroke my back gently. "Amazing," he agreed.

I smiled, my body still humming with the aftermath of our lovemaking. "It was everything I hoped it would be," I said softly. "And more."

We lay there for a while, our bodies entwined, our hearts beating in sync. The rain continued to fall outside, a soothing lullaby that seemed to echo the contentment I felt inside.

With a sigh, I rolled to the side.

"We're not done yet, sweetheart," Jackson said. "Now it's my turn."

CHAPTER 6

The rain persisted, a steady drumbeat against the cabin roof as I lay there with Regina's warm body nestled against mine. The storm outside was nothing compared to the tempest of emotions swirling within me. I had never felt so completely consumed, so utterly connected to another person—or, in this case, two people—in my entire life.

Harley's steady breaths on the other side of Regina told me he was still recuperating. We were both lost in our thoughts, both processing the intensity of what we had just shared. The memory sent a shiver of desire coursing through me, reigniting the fire that had barely begun to smolder.

Harley had experienced Regina, but now it was my turn, and I ached to feel my cock sheathed in her body.

A flash of lightning illuminated the room, casting long, dancing shadows on the walls. Regina stirred, her body pressing closer to mine, her ass grazing against my growing erection. I stifled a groan, trying not to disturb her, but it was too late. She turned her head, her eyes meeting mine in the dim light.

"Jackson," she whispered, her voice husky with desire. "You said it was your turn. I'm ready. I need you inside me, now."

I nodded, brushing a strand of hair away from her face. Those sapphire eyes seemed to see deep into my soul and knew what I needed.

"Yes," I said, knowing that was exactly where I wanted to be.

She smiled softly, her hand reaching up to cup my cheek.

Harley shifted behind her, his hand tracing lazy patterns on her hip. This time, I would claim her. I would make her mine.

Regina's breath hitched as Harley's hand dipped lower, his fingers brushing against the sensitive skin of her inner thigh. She turned to look at him, her eyes widening as she felt his desire pressing against her. "Harley... Jackson..." she whispered, her voice filled with longing. "I want... I need..."

I leaned in, my lips capturing hers in a soft, slow kiss. I could taste her desire, could feel it in the way her body melted into mine.

"What do you need, Regina?" I murmured against her lips. "Tell us."

She hesitated, her cheeks flushing with embarrassment. "I want to taste you," she said softly, her eyes flicking between Harley and me. "Both of you. And I want you to taste me. I want to feel your mouths on me, your tongues... everywhere."

Her words sent a jolt of lust straight to my groin. The thought of her mouth on me, of her sweetness on my tongue, was almost more than I could bear. I looked at Harley, saw the same desire reflected in his eyes. We both wanted this, wanted her, more than anything.

I shifted, moving to lie on my back as Regina sat up, her eyes locked onto mine. She leaned down, her lips trailing soft kisses down my chest and stomach, her hands tracing the lines of my muscles. My heart pounded in my chest and the anticipation built as she moved lower and lower.

While in the Navy, how many times had I dreamed of this? Longed for this, ached for the touch of her mouth on my cock? Usually, I lay in my bunk, jacking off, but now it was going to happen for real.

And then her mouth was on me, her lips soft and warm as they wrapped around my cock. I groaned, my hips lifting off the bed as she took me deeper, her tongue swirling around my shaft. The sensation was incredible, a mix of pleasure and torture that left me gasping for breath.

My dreams were nothing compared to the real experience.

Harley moved behind her, his hands gripping her hips as he guided her onto her hands and knees. She moaned around my cock as he pressed a kiss to the small of her back, his hands sliding down to cup her ass. He trailed kisses down her spine, his tongue darting out to taste her skin, his teeth scraping gently against her sensitive flesh.

Regina's body shivered with pleasure as Harley's mouth moved lower, his tongue tracing a path down the crack of her ass, down to her sweet, wet pussy. She gasped, her mouth releasing my cock as she cried out in pleasure. I reached down, my fingers tangling in her hair as I guided her mouth back to me, my hips thrusting gently into her willing mouth.

I wouldn't last long this way. Her sweet mouth was driving me closer and closer to the edge.

Harley's tongue found her clit, circling and teasing as his fingers slid inside her. Regina moaned, her body writhing with pleasure as we both worked to drive her wild. I could feel her pleasure building, could feel the tension in her body as she neared the edge.

But I didn't want her to come like this. I wanted to taste her, to feel her release on my tongue. I gently pulled her away from my cock, ignoring her soft whimper of protest.

"Not yet, sweetheart," I murmured, shifting so I lay beneath her, my head between her thighs.

Harley moved to her side, his cock replacing mine in her mouth. She moaned, her body trembling with anticipation as I pressed a soft kiss to her inner thigh. I smelled her arousal, saw the evidence of her desire glistening on her skin. I leaned in, my tongue tracing a slow, deliberate path up her thigh, closer and closer to her center.

A shiver racked her body, and I deliberately slowed my tongue, making her anticipate my next move.

She cried out as my tongue found her clit, her body bucking against my mouth. I gripped her hips, holding her steady as I explored her with my tongue, tasting her sweetness, feeling her body respond to my touch. Harley's groans of pleasure mingled with Regina's, the sound of their desire filling the room, spurring me on.

I slid two fingers inside her, feeling her body clench around me as I began to move, my fingers thrusting in and out of her in time with the movements of my tongue. She was close, so close, her body trembling with the effort of holding back her release.

Harley's hand fisted in her hair, his hips thrusting into her mouth as he neared his own release. "Regina," he gasped. "I'm close. I'm so fucking close."

His words seemed to push her over the edge. She cried out, her body convulsing as her orgasm hit, her sweetness flooding my tongue as she came undone. I lapped up every last drop of her pleasure, my own body aching with the need for release.

Harley followed suit, his body tensing as he found his release in her mouth. She swallowed every last bit of him, her body still trembling with the aftershocks of her own pleasure.

She collapsed onto the bed, her body boneless and sated. I moved to lie beside her, my cock aching with the need for release. But I wanted to take my time, wanted to savor this moment, this connection. Wanted to relish these moments.

I trailed my fingers lightly over her body, tracing patterns on her skin as I explored every dip, every curve. She shivered, her body responding to my touch even in her exhausted state. I leaned in, my lips capturing hers in a soft, slow kiss. I could taste Harley on her lips, could taste her own pleasure, and the combination was intoxicating.

Harley lay on her other side, his hand reaching out to stroke her body, his fingers brushing against mine. We both explored her, our touches synchronized, our desire for her palpable. She moaned softly, her body arching into our touch, her need for us evident.

I trailed my hand down her body, my fingers finding her clit once more. She gasped, her body jerking with the sudden sensitivity. I circled her gently, my touch featherlight, coaxing her body back to life. Her breath hitched, her hips lifting to meet my touch as her desire began to build once more.

Harley's hand moved to her breast, his fingers teasing her nipple, his touch firm and insistent. She cried out, her body writhing as we both worked to drive her wild. I could feel her pleasure building, feel the tension in her body as she neared the edge once more.

But this time, I didn't want her to come alone. I wanted to feel her body clench around me, wanted to feel her pleasure as

I found my own release. I shifted, moving to lie between her legs, my cock poised at her entrance.

She looked up at me, her eyes filled with desire and lust. "Jackson," she whispered. "I want you."

Her words sent a surge of emotion coursing through me, a mix of heat and desire that left me breathless. I leaned down, my lips capturing hers in a deep, passionate kiss as I slid inside her, her body welcoming me, embracing me, completing me.

My hips thrust forward, my body claiming hers as she claimed mine. Harley's hand moved to her thigh, his fingers gripping her flesh as he guided her leg up, opening her to me completely. She cried out, her body writhing beneath mine as I drove deeper and deeper into her.

I felt her body clench around me as she neared the end. I leaned down, my lips capturing her nipple, my teeth scraping gently against her sensitive flesh. She gasped, her body arching into mine as she finally let go, her orgasm crashing over her like a wave.

"Jackson," she screamed.

I followed her over the edge, my own release exploding through me as I filled her with my seed. I cried out her name, my body convulsing with the force of my pleasure, my heart pounding in my chest.

We collapsed in a tangle of limbs, our bodies slick with sweat, our breaths coming in ragged gasps. This was where I belonged, here with Regina and Harley, in this moment of perfect intimacy and connection.

As we lay there, our bodies entwined, our hearts beating in sync, I knew this was just the beginning. There were still so many things to figure out, so many challenges to face. But with Regina by my side, with Harley by my side, we could conquer anything. Together, we could heal the wounds of the past and build a future filled with love and happiness. Together, we could weather any storm.

If only what I wanted was what they wanted as well. If only my uncle would vacate the house and land, and we could move in there together. But was Regina ready to commit to us after her last experience?

Was she over the heartbreak called Edward?

CHAPTER 7

The first light of dawn filtered through the cabin window, casting a soft golden hue over the room. I lay there, nestled between Jackson and Harley, their warm bodies pressed against mine, their steady breaths a soothing rhythm in the quiet of the morning. I should have felt content, satiated after a night of passion like no other, but instead, my mind was a whirlwind of confusion and disbelief.

Oh my God, what had I done? It had been less than a week since the botched wedding, and I had jumped into bed with two of my exes. Was I out of my mind?

The question echoed in my brain, a persistent drumbeat I couldn't ignore. I had crossed a line, not just physically but emotionally. I had let them in, both of them, in a way I had sworn I never would again. And now, in the cold light of day, I was desperate to understand what this all meant.

I carefully extricated myself from their embrace, slipping out of bed and wrapping a blanket around my naked body. The cabin was chilly, the storm having left a crisp, autumnal feel to the air. I tiptoed to the kitchen, grateful for the solid wood floor beneath my feet, grounding me in reality.

I set the kettle on the stove, the familiar routine of making coffee a comforting distraction from the chaos in my mind. As I waited for the water to boil, I looked out the window, watching the sun rise over the river. The calm, serene beauty of the scene was a stark contrast to the turmoil inside me.

If I had truly loved Edward, I would not be jumping into bed with Harley and Jackson. And yet, it felt natural. Perfect. Like where I belonged.

The question persisted, gnawing at me like a relentless beast. I had slept with them, both of them, willingly and eagerly. I had reveled in their touch, in the connection we shared, in the overwhelming pleasure they had given me. But now, in the sobering light of day, I was forced to confront the ramifications of my actions.

I was following in the path of my parents, and I'd sworn I would not be like them, but this felt right. All the years of me saying I would never have two lovers, and yet, this morning, my body, my soul, my very being was more complete than ever.

As I poured the hot water over the coffee grounds, the rich aroma filled the small kitchen. With my mug, I sat at the table, wrapping my hands around the warm ceramic, seeking comfort in its heat.

I had always known that Jackson and Harley were dangerous to my heart. Our past was a tumultuous one, filled with love and loss, passion and pain. They had been my first loves, and when they left, they took a piece of me with them. A piece I had never been able to reclaim no matter how hard I tried.

Not even Edward.

And now they were back, and I had let them in again. I opened my heart, my body, my soul to them, and I was terrified of what that meant. Terrified of the power they held over me, terrified of the potential for heartbreak that loomed like a dark cloud on the horizon.

I took a sip of my coffee, the bitter taste grounding me, forcing me to confront the harsh reality of my situation. I had to think and process the whirlwind of emotions that threatened to consume me. I had to figure out what this all meant, what I wanted, and what I truly desired.

A soft creak behind me alerted me that I was no longer alone. I turned to see Jackson standing in the doorway, his hair tousled from sleep, his emerald eyes soft with concern. He was shirtless, his jeans slung low on his hips, and all those muscles screamed for me to touch him. A wave of longing coursed through me, a longing I struggled to suppress.

"Morning," he said softly, his voice a low rumble that sent shivers down my spine. "Couldn't sleep?"

I shook my head, turning back to my coffee, using it as a shield against the intensity of his gaze. "Just needed some time to think," I said, my voice barely above a whisper.

He nodded, understanding in his eyes. He poured himself a cup of coffee and joined me at the table, his presence comforting and unsettling all at once. We sat in silence for a moment, the weight of our shared past and uncertain future hanging heavy in the air.

"Regina," he said finally, his voice filled with a raw emotion that took my breath away. "About last night... I need you to know, it wasn't just... it wasn't just sex for me. For us."

I looked up at him, my heart pounding in my chest. His

eyes were filled with a sincerity that left no room for doubt, a sincerity that both terrified and thrilled me.

"I know," I said softly, my voice barely above a whisper. "What started out as just sex for me evolved. But that's what scares me, Jackson. That's what terrifies me. I don't even know if I'm over my broken engagement, and yet here are the two of you. A temptation that I obviously can't deny. A temptation that helped replace the memories."

He reached out, his hand covering mine, his thumb tracing gentle circles on my skin. "What are you afraid of, Regina?" he asked, his voice filled with a tenderness that brought tears to my eyes.

I took a deep breath, steeling myself for the truth I had been trying to ignore. "I'm afraid of getting hurt again," I admitted, my voice trembling with emotion. "I'm afraid of loving you, of loving both of you and having my heart broken again. I'm afraid of jumping out of one relationship right into another. I don't know if I'm ready. For years, I swore that I would not follow the path of my parents, and yet being with the two of you is making me question everything."

He sighed, his grip on my hand tightening. "Regina, listen to me," he said, his voice filled with fierce determination. "You are enough. You are more than enough. You are everything to me, to us. And I promise you, we are not going anywhere. Our Navy days are behind us. We came home to settle down. And you are who we want. The first person we wanted to see."

His words sent a wave of emotion crashing over me, a mix of hope and fear, longing and doubt. I wanted to believe him, wanted to trust in the promise of his words, in the sincerity of his emotions. But the scars of the past ran deep, and the fear of heartbreak was a powerful force to overcome.

"How can I trust you?" I asked, my voice filled with a vulnerability that left me feeling exposed and raw. "How can I trust that some grand adventure will have the two of you running off again? That's what happened last time. How do I know that what I feel for you isn't just a rebound emotion? This is all so much way too soon. I think I need to pump the brakes."

He looked at me, his eyes filled with a fierce intensity. "You don't know. Only time will show us the answers," he said, his voice filled with conviction. "But our time together was happy. You are who we wanted to see when we arrived home. Imagine how we felt seeing the congratulations banners hanging on the street with your name and Edward's. We were devastated. And then, when we heard what happened, we raced to your parent's house hoping to see you, but you were gone."

She reached out and squeezed his hand. "My mother keeps telling me that things happen for a reason."

"We are in this together, all of us. And we are not going to let you go, not again, not ever, unless you want us to."

His words sent a shiver down my spine, a shiver of longing and hope. I looked up at him, my eyes searching his, seeking the truth in his words, the promise in his eyes. And I saw it, saw the promise of a future filled with love and happiness.

But even as I reveled in the warmth of his words and the sincerity in his gaze, doubt lingered, a persistent, nagging voice in the back of my mind. Could I trust them? Could I trust in the sincerity of their emotions? Could I take that leap of faith, that terrifying, exhilarating plunge into the unknown once again? Especially since I'd just been stood up at the altar.

I looked up at Jackson, my eyes filled with tears, my voice

filled with emotion. "I want this, I want us, more than anything. But I'm not certain I can give you what you need, right now. I need time."

He reached out, his hand cupping my cheek, his thumb brushing away the tears that spilled down my face. "I promise you, Regina," he said, his voice filled with fierce determination. "I promise you that we are in this together, all of us. And we are not going to break your heart. Not this time, not ever. When you're ready, we'll find the answers."

And with those words, with that promise, I felt the weight of my fears, my doubts, my insecurities lifting from my shoulders. Warmth filled me, wrapping around me, enveloping me, cocooning me in a blanket of security and the promise that they would never hurt me again.

I leaned into his touch, my eyes closing, reveling in the sensation of his skin against mine in the comfort of his embrace.

The sound of footsteps behind us alerted me to Harley's presence. I turned to see him standing in the doorway, his eyes filled with a tenderness that took my breath away. He crossed the room in a few quick strides, pulling me into his arms, his lips capturing mine in a deep, passionate kiss.

Pulling back, he gazed into my eyes, and I could feel my body awakening to desire once again. Why was it so instantaneous with these men? What was there between us that I couldn't deny them?

"Don't give up on us," Harley said. "We want you."

Glancing at them nervously, I nodded. "Let's just see what the next few days bring. The creek is still high, so you're not going anywhere. Now, if you'll excuse me, I'm going to get my morning pages written, and then we can do whatever we want to do today."

Walking out of the room, I sighed. I needed a break. A moment alone. How could I be so entwined with these men when I'd just suffered the worst heartache of my life?

But had I really loved Edward, or had he just been convenient?

CHAPTER 8

That evening after dinner, I was ready to go to bed. To wrap Regina in my arms and feel the way her pussy gripped my cock. I knew Jackson felt the same. The memories from last night had stayed with me all day and I was so ready to experience being together again.

The fire crackled in the hearth, casting a warm glow over the rustic living room. We were all comfortably full from dinner, the conversation flowing as smoothly as the wine we've been drinking.

"How about a game of strip poker?" Jackson proposed, leaning back in his chair, his gaze flicking between Regina and me.

I chuckled, watching Regina's cheeks flush a soft pink. She rolled her eyes, but there was a spark of interest there. "Seriously? That's such a cliché," she responded, but her voice lacked conviction.

"Come on, Reggie," I chimed in, using her old nickname deliberately. Today, we'd fallen back into the same rhythm we were accustomed to in high school. Though years had passed, our connection was as strong as ever. "Afraid you'll lose?"

Not one to pass up a competition, she was relenting.

She scoffed, sitting up straighter. "Please, I'll have you both naked before you can say 'fold.'"

Jackson grinned, standing to grab a deck of cards from the drawer. "Game on, then."

We settled around the coffee table, the fire warming our sides. Regina dealt the first hand, her fingers deftly shuffling the cards. I watched her, the firelight dancing off her blonde hair, her sapphire eyes gleaming with competitive spirit. She'd always been a sight to behold, but tonight, she was breathtaking.

How had we gotten so lucky to get a second chance with her?

The game started innocently enough. Jackson lost the first round and dramatically removed his sock, tossing it aside with a laugh. Regina lost the next, shrugging out of her sweater to reveal a simple white tank top underneath. I swallowed hard, my eyes lingering on the swell of her breasts. Remembering the way they felt, their taste, and wanting another chance at them.

"That was pure luck," Regina said. "Next time, I'll get you."

"Oh, darling, I want you to get me in every possible way," Jackson said laughing.

A few more rounds passed, the tension building as more clothes were shed. Jackson was down to his jeans, Regina was in her tank top and panties, and I was left in my boxers and T-shirt. The air was thick with anticipation, the earlier teasing banter replaced with heated glances and loaded silences.

"My call," she said and all I could think about was how I was ready for the cards to end and the playing to begin.

Regina dealt another hand, her eyes meeting mine over the cards. I could see the desire there, the want. She licked her lips, a small gesture that sent a jolt of lust straight to my groin. I was hard, painfully so, and I knew she could see the tent in my boxers.

"I fold," I said.

Her brows raise in a questioning way.

Standing, I pulled off my T-shirt. Regina's eyes roam over my chest, her breath hitching slightly. I smirk, sitting back down, my erection straining against my boxers.

Jackson won the next round, his grin wide as he looked at Regina. "Off with it, sweetheart," he drawled, nodding at her tank top.

She hesitated for a moment, then pulled it off in one swift movement. Her breasts spilled out, nipples hardening under our gazes. My mouth went dry, my heart pounding in my chest. I wanted to touch her, to taste her.

"To hell with this game," I said, reaching for her.

The game was forgotten after that. Regina wrapped her hand around my length over my boxers. I groaned, bucking into her touch. Jackson moved behind her, his hands cupping her breasts, his thumbs circling her nipples. She moaned, her head falling back onto his shoulder.

I shucked off my boxers. My cock sprang free, eager for her touch. Regina looked at me, her eyes dark with desire. She leaned forward, her tongue flicking out to lick the pre-cum beading at the tip. I hissed, my hands fisting in her hair.

Just that simple touch was enough to send my blood pounding in rhythm with my heart.

She took me into her mouth, her head bobbing as she worked me deeper. Jackson's hands roamed over her body, one slipping between her legs. She moaned around my cock, the vibrations sending shocks of pleasure through me.

I pulled her off me, not wanting to come too soon. She pouted, looking up at me with those big eyes. I smirked, pushing her gently onto her back. "Your turn," I murmured, spreading her legs wide.

Her panties were soaked, clinging to her folds. I pulled them off, tossing them aside. She was pink and glistening, her clit swollen and begging for attention. I dove in, my tongue licking a long stripe up her center. She cried out, her hips bucking.

Jackson kneeled beside her, his fingers finding her nipples again. He rolled them between his fingers, pinching and pulling until she was writhing beneath us. I slipped two fingers inside her, crooking them to hit that sweet spot. She gasped, her inner walls clenching around me.

"Harley," she panted, her hands fisting in my hair. "Please..."

I chuckled, pulling back slightly. "Please, what, baby?"

"Make me cum," she begged, her eyes wild. "Please make me cum."

I grinned, lowering my head again. My tongue flicked against her clit, my fingers pumping in and out of her. She was so wet, so responsive.

"Harley," she screamed, her orgasm crashing over her.

As she came down, I flipped her onto her stomach. She looked back at me, a questioning look in her eyes. I rubbed my hands over her ass, squeezing her firm cheeks.

"Ever had a spanking, baby?" I asked, my voice low.

She bit her lip, shaking her head. I grinned, bringing my hand down on her ass with a sharp smack. She yelped, her eyes widening in surprise. I rubbed the sting away, soothing her.

"Too much?" I asked, my heart pounding. I needed her to like this, to want this. I needed to mix a little pain in with her pleasure.

She shook her head, a small smile playing on her lips. "More," she whispered.

I was happy to oblige. I spanked her again, harder this time. She moaned, pushing back into my hand. I saw her pussy glistening and wet, begging for more. Her sweet little ass cheeks were pink, and I liked seeing my handprint on her backside.

No, I didn't want to hurt her, but I wanted her to experience everything and I wanted to be the one to give her pleasure.

Jackson moved beside me, his fingers slipping into her folds. She groaned, spreading her legs wider. He pumped his fingers in and out of her, his thumb brushing against her clit.

"She's so wet, Harley," he murmured, his voice hoarse. "I think she likes it."

I chuckled, spanking her again. This time, Jackson slipped his fingers out of her pussy, tracing them up to her ass. She tensed slightly as he circled her tight hole, but she didn't stop him.

"Easy, baby," I soothed, rubbing her back. "Just relax."

Jackson slid a finger inside her ass, slowly working it in and out. Regina's body relaxed into the sensation. I spanked her again, the sound of flesh on flesh filling the room.

"God, that's hot," Jackson groaned, his cock hard and ready. "Grab the lube, Harley. Let's make this more interesting."

I nodded, reaching for the small bag I'd brought down earlier and pulled out the lube. I coat my fingers, replacing Jackson's in her ass. She moaned, pushing back against me. I worked her slowly, stretching her.

Jackson moved in front of her, his cock at her mouth. She took him eagerly, her head bobbing as she sucked him deep. The sight of her on her hands and knees, sucking Jackson off while I fingered her ass, was almost too much.

I slipped a second finger inside her, scissoring them to stretch her further. She moaned around Jackson's cock, her body trembling. I could tell she was close, her orgasm building.

Jackson pulled out of her mouth, his breath coming in ragged gasps. "Fuck, I'm close," he groaned.

I nodded, pulling my fingers out of her ass. I grabbed the butt plug from the same bag as the lube and coated it. "Ready, baby?" I asked, pressing the tip against her.

She nodded, her eyes dark with desire. I slowly pushed the plug inside her, her body tensing and then relaxing as it slipped in. She moaned, her body adjusting to the sensation.

"God, that feels good," she panted, her eyes closing.

I smiled and spanked her ass again. "And this?" I asked, slipping my fingers into her pussy.

Her breath hitched. "Yes," she gasped. "God, yes."

Jackson moved behind her, his cock replacing my fingers. He thrust into her, her body rocking with each movement. I shifted in front of her, my cock aching for her touch. She took me into her mouth, her eyes locked onto mine.

The room was filled with the sound of our moans, our bodies moving in sync. I could feel my orgasm building, my body tensing. Regina's mouth was hot and wet, her tongue working magic on my cock.

While I really wished we could make this last longer, I was close to coming.

Jackson groaned, his body stiffening. "Fuck, I'm coming," he gasped, his hips jerking as he spilled into her.

Regina whimpered, her own orgasm crashing over her. Her body convulsed, her inner walls clenching around Jackson. The sight of her lost in pleasure sent me over the edge. I came hard, my cock pulsing in her mouth.

And my girl, she swallowed all of my seed.

We collapsed in a tangle of limbs, our breaths coming in ragged gasps. The fire crackled beside us, casting a warm glow over our sweat-slicked bodies. Regina looked up at me, a soft smile on her lips.

"That was..." she started, her voice trailing off.

I grinned, pulling her into my arms. "Hot?" I suggested.

She laughed, snuggling against my chest. "Very hot," she agreed.

"How does the butt plug feel?" I asked not wanting her to suffer from it, but knowing it was a vital part of making her available to both of us without hurting her.

"It fills me up," she said.

"I'll say," Jackson replied. "You were so tight. I can't wait until both of us are taking you at the same time."

Jackson's arms wrapped around both of us. We lay there, our bodies entwined, the fire warming our skin. In this moment, everything felt right. The past was forgotten, the future uncertain, but right now, we had each other. And that was enough.

As the fire died down, we moved to the bedroom, our bodies still tangled together. We made love again, slower this time, exploring each other's bodies with soft touches and gentle kisses. Regina fell asleep in our arms, her body sated and her heart, hopefully, a little bit healed.

As I drifted off to sleep, I couldn't help but feel a sense of contentment wash over me. This, right here, was what I'd been missing. The connection, the intimacy, the growing sense of love. I wasn't going to let it slip away again. Not without a fight.

Tomorrow, we'd talk. We'd figure out where we went from here. But for now, I was going to enjoy this feeling. This sense of rightness, of belonging. Because after all these years, all the pain, and the heartache, we were finally where we were meant to be.

Together.

CHAPTER 9

After a couple days of the ground drying out, I helped prepare a fire out near the creek with Harley and Regina. I felt more relaxed and better than I had in years. The sun dipped below the horizon, casting the sky in hues of orange and pink.

We'd been holed up in the cabin for days, our bodies entwined, our hearts slowly mending. But tonight, we craved the open sky, the crackle of fire, and the taste of roasted marshmallows.

I gathered firewood from the nearby forest, the scent of pine filling my nostrils. Harley and Regina worked together to set up a circle of stones, their laughter echoing through the clearing. This, right here, was what I missed. The camaraderie and the simple joy of being together.

We'd been so young, so close, and so not ready to make a commitment to one another when we were in high school. And our foolish actions had hurt Regina so badly. But now we were making it up to her, and if she would have us, there would be no need for another man.

As I dropped the wood into the pit, my phone rang. My attorney Nathan's name flashed on the screen. I stepped away to answer, leaving Harley and Regina to start the fire.

"Jackson," Nathan greeted, his voice gruff. "I've got news."

I braced myself, my heart pounding. "Good or bad?"

He chuckled. "Good, for once. The eviction notice has been served. Your uncle has ten days to vacate the property."

Relief washed over me, so intense it left me breathless. "That's... that's great, Nathan. Thank you."

"Don't thank me yet," he warned. "He's not going down without a fight. Be prepared for that. If he refutes the eviction notice, we could find ourselves in court."

That was an understatement. Uncle Martin was never one to go down without a fight.

I nodded, my gaze flicking to Regina. She was laughing at something Harley said, her face glowing in the firelight. I'll do whatever it took to protect her, to protect us. "I'm prepared for any fight he wants to bring."

"Well, I just wanted you to know the good news."

"Thanks, Nathan."

I hung up, tucking the phone into my pocket. When I returned to the fire, Regina looked up at me, her eyes questioning. "Everything okay?" she asked.

I smiled, taking a seat beside her. "Better than okay. The eviction notice has been served. My uncle has to leave."

Harley whooped, clapping me on the back. "That's fantastic, man."

Regina smiled, leaning into me. "What eviction notice? You haven't told me about this."

For the next five minutes, I filled her in on the shenanigans my uncle was trying to pull.

"I asked my uncle to look after the ranch while I was in the Navy. And now, he's refusing to leave."

Regina shook her head. "Family. Love them, hate them, they can cause lots of problems. I'm glad, Jackson. Truly."

"Not your family," Harley said.

"No, not mine," she said.

Her family had been the envy of my life and every kid who knew them.

We settled into a comfortable silence, the fire crackling before us. Above, the stars began to peek out, the moon casting a soft glow over the landscape. It's beautiful, peaceful. A far cry from the chaos of our past.

Harley broke the silence, his voice soft. "Remember our first camping trip together?" he asked, looking at Regina.

She laughed, her eyes sparkling with the memory. "How could I forget? We were what, sixteen? Thought we were so grown up, sneaking out with a case of beer."

I chuckled, the memory playing in my mind. "We ended up telling ghost stories until dawn. Scared ourselves so bad, we couldn't sleep."

Regina shivered, cuddling closer to me. "I still can't walk by the old mill without thinking of the Headless Horseman."

Harley grinned, poking the fire with a stick. "Those were good times," he said, his voice tinged with nostalgia.

"They were," I agreed. "But I don't miss the Navy."

Regina looked up at me, her eyes curious. "What was it like? Being a Navy SEAL?"

I sighed, staring into the fire. "Tough. Brutal, even. The training alone... it breaks most men. But it made us stronger, made us brothers."

Harley nodded, his expression somber. "We saw things, did things... things that change a man."

Regina reached out, taking his hand. "Is that where you got this?" she asked, tracing the scar that ran near his temple.

He smiled, a bitter twist of his lips. "Yes, though I like to tell people I got it in a bar fight. That sounds more intriguing than a war wound."

I laughed, the sound echoing through the night. "You have no idea, Regina. The shit we'd get into... it's a miracle we made it out alive."

Her smile faded, her expression turning serious. "But it wasn't without continued injuries, was it?"

The woman had noticed Harley's quiet responses, his headaches, the way he would zone out sometimes. I worried about him. Though we were not related by blood, he was still my brother.

Harley and I exchanged a look. We'd never talked about his injuries, not with her, not with anyone. But she deserved to know, to understand.

Harley took a deep breath, his eyes locked onto the fire. "I got injured on our last mission. A concussion, a bad one. I'd had a few before, but this one... it messed me up. I still get headaches, and sometimes I black out. The Navy gave me a medical discharge."

Regina's eyes widened, her hand tightening around his. "Harley, I'm so sorry."

He shrugged, a small smile on his lips. "It is what it is, baby. I'm just glad to be out, to be here with you."

She leaned into him, her head resting on his shoulder. "Me too," she whispered.

I watched them, a warmth spreading through my chest. This was what we fought for, what we dreamed of during those long, brutal nights: a chance to come home, to be with her, not knowing if she would still be single or even give us a second chance.

Regina glanced up at me, her eyes soft. "Remember the first time we made love?" she asked, her voice barely above a whisper.

How could we not? "By the campfire," I murmured. "Just like this."

A sweet, delicious memory of our first time. It was right before we told her we were leaving for the Navy. She'd been crushed. And that was when the problems started.

She smiled, her cheeks flushing pink. "I was so nervous. But you... you both made it so perfect."

Harley's hand cupped her cheek. "And we always will make it perfect for you."

She turned to him, her lips brushing against his. I watched them, my body stirring. When she pulled back, her eyes met mine, dark with desire. She leaned in, her lips finding mine. She tasted like marshmallows and smoke, sweet and intoxicating.

I deepened the kiss, my hands tangling in her hair. She moaned, her body pressing against mine. I felt her heart pounding, her breath coming in ragged gasps. I wanted her, needed her. But not yet. Tonight was about more than just sex. It was about healing and reconnecting.

She pulled back, her eyes locked onto mine. "Fuck me," she whispered. "Both of you."

I stood and held out my hand, helping her to her feet. Harley followed, his eyes dark with desire. We led her to the blanket we spread out earlier, our bodies pressed close to hers.

We undressed her slowly, our hands exploring every curve, every dip. She was soft and warm, her skin glowing in the firelight. She was beautiful, perfect in her imperfection.

Harley laid her down, his body covering hers. He kissed her, his hands roaming over her body. I watched them, my cock hard and aching. But I waited, letting him have this moment.

He pulled back, his eyes meeting mine. I nodded, taking his place. I kissed her, my tongue slipping into her mouth. She moaned, her body arching against mine. I felt her heart pounding, her breath coming in ragged gasps.

I trailed my lips down her neck, her collarbone, her breasts. I took one nipple into my mouth, sucking gently. Her hands fisted in my hair. I tasted her wetness, her desire. She was ready, but I wanted to take my time, to savor this moment.

Harley moved beside me, his hands trailing down her stomach, her hips, her thighs. He spread her legs, his fingers slipping into her folds. She gasped, her body bucking. He worked her slowly.

My lips trailed kisses over her stomach, down her body. I smelled her arousal, sweet and intoxicating. I wanted to consume her, to feel her come against my mouth.

I settled between her legs, my tongue flicking out to taste her. Her hips bucked as my tongue touched her swollen clitoris, and I gripped her thighs, holding her still as I explored her wet folds. She tasted sweet and tangy, her addictive flavor making my mouth water. Regina reached out to Harley, wrapping her hand around his hard, throbbing cock. He groaned in pleasure, his head falling back as she stroked him in time with my licks.

My tongue continued to dance over her clit while I slid a finger inside her, curling it upward to massage the sensitive spot within. She moaned louder, her body arching toward me. I could feel her inner muscles clench around my finger as she came, and I lapped up every drop of her juices that spilled onto my waiting tongue. My cock throbbed with need, but I held off, savoring the moment.

Harley's cock replaced my tongue as he plunged into her wet heat. Regina's back arched and she moaned louder still as he thrust into her rhythmically. He grabbed her hips for leverage, driving himself deeper with each powerful stroke. He was a sight to behold—my best friend and lover, taking my kindergarten crush apart with abandonment.

I positioned myself at the entrance of Regina's face, aching for relief. She took me eagerly into her warm mouth, sucking me deep as she bobbed her head up and down in time with Harley's thrusts. It was the hottest thing I'd ever seen—the three of us tangled together in this erotic dance of

The sight of Regina completely absorbed in pleasure was too much for me to handle. Lost in passion, I reached the point of no return and released myself into her mouth with powerful pulses. She swallowed every drop without breaking eye contact.

Harley's body tensed as he neared his own climax. "Fuck, I'm coming," he gasped through gritted teeth, his hips jerking with involuntary spasms as he released himself deep inside Regina.

We fell into a twisted heap of limbs and heavy breathing – our bodies sticky with sweat. Regina looked up at me through half-lidded eyes, a soft smile playing at the corners of her lips.

"I'm happy. Really happy," she said smiling at us.

"Not as much as I am," I said.

Harley chuckled. "Best sex of my life."

CHAPTER 10

The water cascaded over me, hot and steamy, as I stood under the showerhead. The cabin's water pressure was a joke, but right now, the weak stream suits my mood. I was tender in places I hadn't been in years, a delicious ache that reminded me of the night before. The campfire, the stories, the lovemaking. It was perfect. Too perfect.

I squirted some of my favorite shower gel onto my loofah and began to scrub at my skin as if I could wash away the uncertainty that had crept into my mind. What was I doing? I came to the mountains to escape, to heal, not to fall back into the arms of the two men who broke my heart all those years ago.

I closed my eyes, letting the water run over my face. Images of last night floated behind my eyelids – the firelight dancing on Jackson's and Harley's faces as they laughed and shared stories. The taste of marshmallows and smoke on their lips. The feel of their hands, their bodies, their hearts beating in sync with mine.

A sob caught in my throat. I couldn't do this. I couldn't let them back in. I'd just come out of a disastrous engagement. I should've been focusing on myself, on rebuilding my life, not jumping into bed with my past.

But it felt so right, so natural like no time had passed. Like we were meant to be together.

I shook my head, trying to dislodge the thoughts. No. I wouldn't go down this road again. I wouldn't set myself up for more heartache. I'd had enough of that to last a lifetime.

I turned off the shower and stepped out, wrapping a towel around myself. The cabin was quiet, the guys still asleep. I tiptoed to the bedroom, my eyes lingering on their forms huddled under the blankets. Jackson's arm was thrown over Harley, his hand resting on Harley's chest. They look so peaceful, so content.

A pang of longing hit me so sharply it took my breath away. I wanted that. I wanted to wake up every morning to their warmth, their love. But I was terrified. Terrified of being left behind again. Terrified of not being enough. Terrified of standing in the church alone once again.

I dressed quickly, pulling on a pair of jeans and a sweatshirt. I needed to get out of here to clear my head. I scribbled a note, leaving it on the kitchen table. "Gone for a walk. Be back later."

The morning air was crisp, the sun barely peeking over the horizon. I hugged my arms around myself, setting off at a brisk pace. The leaves crunched under my feet, the sound echoing through the quiet forest. It was peaceful out here. Calm. Just what I needed.

I walked aimlessly, my mind a whirlwind of thoughts and emotions. I thought about Edward, about the wedding that never was. I was so focused on the fairy tale, on the idea of love, that I ignored the red flags. I ignored the coldness in his eyes, the calculating smirk, and how he always made me feel like I was lacking. The way his family wouldn't accept mine and chose to look down their noses at us.

I wouldn't make that mistake again. I wouldn't ignore my instincts or my heart for the sake of a fantasy.

But was that what I was doing with Jackson and Harley? Ignoring reality for the sake of a memory? We were young when we were together dating the last year of high school. We'd all changed. How can I be sure that what we had then will translate to now?

And what about their lives? They'd been in the military, seen things, done things that I couldn't even imagine. Could they truly settle down and be happy with a simple life in the town I refuse to leave again?

With Edward, I'd agreed to stay in Austin, but no more. Nothing was taking me away from my family and the town I loved.

I sighed, running a hand through my hair. This was what I always did. I overthought. I overanalyzed. I found every reason why something wouldn't work, why I wasn't good enough. It was a defense mechanism, a way to protect myself from getting hurt.

But it was also a way to keep myself from living. From taking chances, from following my heart.

I stopped walking, looking around. I ended up at the river, the same spot where I was fishing when the guys showed up. The water rippled over the rocks, the sound soothing and calming. I sat on a large boulder, letting the peacefulness of the scene wash over me.

In the last two days, the creek had gone back to its normal height. The guys could leave anytime, and yet I was enjoying them being here with me.

I thought about what Jackson said last night, about how they'd changed, how they were not the same young, stupid teens they were. I thought about Harley, about the pain in his eyes when he talked about his injury and discharge. They'd been through so much, seen so much. But they were here, they were trying.

And so was I. I was trying to heal, to move on, to find my place in the world. Maybe, just maybe, our paths had crossed again for a reason. Maybe we were meant to heal together.

But that meant taking a risk, putting my heart on the line. And I wasn't sure I was ready for that. I wasn't sure I could survive another heartbreak.

I sat there for a long time, the sun rising higher in the sky, the world waking up around me. I watched a fish jump, its silvery body catching the light before it splashed back into the water. I listened to the birds chirping, the wind rustling the leaves. I let the beauty of the moment fill me, ground me.

And slowly, surely, I came to a realization. I couldn't keep living in fear. I couldn't keep hiding from love and life because I was scared of getting hurt. I had to take chances. I had to put myself out there because that was the only way to truly live.

Yes, I'd been badly burned. But these men were the first ones to capture my heart so many years ago. And maybe we wouldn't last forever, but right now, I had to give them a chance. To let them into my heart. To trust them.

I stood, my mind made up. I was going to talk to Jackson and Harley. I would tell them how I felt, what I wanted. And if they wanted the same thing, then we'd figure it out. Together.

As I turned to leave, I heard voices. Loud, angry voices. I froze, my heart pounding. It was Jackson and Harley. And they were arguing.

I moved closer, hiding behind a tree. I shouldn't eavesdrop, but I couldn't help myself. I needed to know what they were saying.

"These past few days have been wonderful," Jackson said. "But I'm afraid. I'm afraid she's not ready. I'm afraid you're not ready, and I fear my own emotions."

"She deserves the truth," Harley countered. "She needs to know we love her and want to be with her. And then she deserves to make her own choice."

I gasped, my hand flying to my mouth. They loved me. They wanted to be with me. But they were scared, just like I was. They were worried about hurting me, about not being good enough.

I stepped out from behind the tree, my heart pounding. "I already know," I said, my voice steady and strong.

They turned to look at me, their eyes wide with surprise. "Regina—" Jackson started.

"I know you're scared," I said. "I know you're worried about hurting me. But I also know I want to be with you. But I need to know you want the same thing. That you're willing to take this chance, to fight for us."

They looked at each other, then back at me. And in their eyes, I saw the answer. I saw the desire, the determination.

"We do," Harley said, his voice firm. "We want to be with you, Regina. We want to fight for us. What we have together is special. It's worth fighting for."

A breeze blew, scattering pine needles.

"But we need to be honest," Jackson added. "We need to talk about the future, about what we want, what we need. We need to make sure this is right, that this is what we all want."

A smile spread across my face. "I agree. But first, I think we need to go back to the cabin. I think we need to talk, to really talk. About everything."

They nodded, their faces serious. But I saw the hope in their eyes, the same hope that was blooming in my chest. We were going to do this. We were going to fight for us. Together.

As we walked back to the cabin, hand in hand, I felt a sense of peace wash over me. This was right. This was what I wanted. This was what I'd been missing.

In the house, Harley and I settled on the couch, with Jackson in the chair, each with a cup of coffee in hand.

"Who wants to go first?" Jackson asked.

"I do," I said. It was time for me to confess everything.

"We went on that camping trip together toward the end of school," I said, remembering how hurt I'd been when I learned they were leaving. "We made love for the first time. We spoke of love to one another and then when we returned home, you guys told me the truth. That you had signed up for the Navy and were leaving in three days to go to basic training. I was devastated."

"And angry," Harley said.

"I'd just given you my virginity, and you were leaving. What if I'd been pregnant?"

The idiots glanced at one another.

"Were you?"

"No," I said, remembering how scared I'd been. "But if I had been, you were gone."

Harley sighed. "We were young and stupid and wanted to experience life outside of Blessing."

"Why didn't you tell me you were leaving sooner?"

"We had planned on telling you while we were out camping, but then we made love, and neither one of us had the heart to tell you. We didn't want to end the weekend with us telling you good-bye," Jackson said.

And yet, that was almost exactly what had happened.

When we had gotten home, they'd finally come clean and told me they were shipping out. Three days until my heart was shattered.

"You stopped taking our calls," Harley said.

"Yes, I did," I replied. "I felt like I'd been used."

"No," Jackson responded angrily. "No, what happened between us was spontaneous and beautiful, and we didn't plan on having sex that night. Hell, we didn't bring condoms with us, if you remember."

"No, you didn't, and neither did I. That's why I was so afraid I was pregnant," I said, recalling how I'd waited anxiously for my period.

"What can we do to keep this from happening again?" Harley asked.

"We have to trust one another," Jackson said.

"You need to talk to me. Tell me what is going on. Your plans affect me if we're going to make this relationship work. Run off and leave me again, as you did before, and this is over for good."

"Never," Harley said.

"Never," Jackson replied.

After that, the tension between us seemed to ease. We spent the rest of the day talking—about our past, our present, and our future. We talked about our fears, our hopes, and our dreams. We talked about the military, about the things they'd seen and done. We talked about my engagement, about Edward, about the wedding that never was.

We talked until our voices were hoarse, until our eyes were heavy with exhaustion. But we talked. And it felt good. It felt right.

Jackson stood, taking my hand. "Regina, we want to be with you. We want to build a life with you. But we need to know that you want the same thing. That you're willing to take this chance, to fight for us."

I looked up at him, my heart swelling. I wasn't ready to say *I love you*, but my heart was so involved that I knew the words were building there, growing with the emotions I felt. "I want to be with you, both of you. I want to fight for us."

Harley stood, taking my other hand. "Then we're in this together. The three of us. No matter what."

I smiled, my heart so full it felt like it might burst. "Together," I agreed. "No matter what."

And as we stood there, our hands outstretched, me holding onto each man's palm, the sun setting behind us, the future uncertain but full of promise, I knew this is right. This was what I wanted. This was where I belonged.

CHAPTER 11

The forest floor crunched under our boots as Harley and I walked among the towering pines. The scent of earth and evergreen filled my lungs, grounding me, giving me the courage to voice the thoughts swirling in my mind.

"Do you think it's too soon?" I asked, breaking the comfortable silence that had settled between us.

Harley looked at me, his eyebrows raised. "To ask Regina to marry us?"

I nodded, shoving my hands into my pockets. "Yeah. We've only been back in her life for a few days. What if we're rushing things?"

Harley stopped, leaning against a tree. He gazed out into the distance, his expression thoughtful. "I don't think it's too soon, Jackson. We've known Regina our whole lives. And we've loved her for almost as long."

I sighed, running a hand through my hair. "I know. But we hurt her, Harley. We left her. What if she's not ready to trust us again? Not like that?"

Harley's expression softened, and he clapped a hand on my

shoulder. "She's ready, Jackson. You saw her these past few days. She's happy. She laughs, she jokes, she…smiles."

I smiled, thinking about Regina's laughter, her warmth, her strength. She'd become a beacon of light in our lives, a light that had been missing for far too long. "You're right," I said. "I just... I don't want to screw this up."

Harley gave my shoulder a squeeze. "We won't. We'll do this right. We'll make her happy, Jackson. Every day for the rest of our lives."

I took a deep breath, determination settling in my gut. "All right. Let's do this. Let's make a special dinner while she's down at the creek. Something she'll love. And then... and then we ask her."

Harley's eyes shined with excitement and nervousness. "Sounds like a plan. All she can do is say no."

We turned back toward the cabin, our steps quick and purposeful. As we approached, I started planning the dinner based on what I'd seen in the fridge. Steak, maybe. Regina loved steak. And potatoes. And maybe some of that corn on the cob she liked so much.

Harley interrupted my thoughts, his voice low. "You think we should call her dads? Ask for their blessing?"

I glanced at him, surprised. "You want to do this old-school?"

He shrugged, a slight blush on his cheeks. "I just think... I think they'd appreciate it. And I think Regina would too."

I was touched by his thoughtfulness. "We'll call them. But first, let's get dinner started. I want it to be ready when Regina gets back."

We reached the cabin, the familiar warmth and comfort wrapping around us as we stepped inside. I headed straight to the kitchen, pulling out ingredients and cookware. Harley disappeared into the bedroom, murmuring something about needing to look nice for dinner.

I was seasoning the steaks when a knock came at the door. I frowned, glancing at the clock.

Harley emerged from the bedroom, dressed in a nice button-down shirt and jeans. He caught my eye and raised an eyebrow. I shrugged, nodding toward the door. "You want to get that?"

He walked over, his steps confident and sure. But when he opened the door, his entire body stiffened. I saw his back straighten and his shoulders tense. And I knew even before he spoke that something is wrong.

The visitor spoke. "Hi, I'm Edward. Is Regina here?"

My heart stopped. Edward. Regina's ex-fiancé. The man who left her at the altar. The man who broke her heart. What was he doing here?

I wiped my hands on a dish towel, moving to stand beside Harley, ready to kick his ass. Edward looked up at us, his expression smug and self-assured. He was dressed in a fancy suit, his hair slicked back, his eyes cold and calculating.

"Gentlemen," he says, nodding at us. "I'm here to see Regina. I believe she and I have some unfinished business."

Anger surged through me, hot and fierce. I took a step forward, but Harley's hand on my arm stopped me. "Regina's not here," he said, his voice deceptively calm. "And even if she was, she wouldn't want to see you."

Edward smirked, his eyes flicking between us. "Oh, really? You two seem awfully confident about that. But from what I hear, Regina and I had a... misunderstanding. I'm here to clear that up."

I scoffed, disbelief coloring my voice. "A misunderstanding? You left her at the altar, you asshole. There's no misunderstanding that."

Edward's smirk faded, his expression turning hard. "That's between me and Regina. And it's none of your business."

Harley stepped forward, his voice low and threatening. "Everything about Regina is our business. She's ours. And you're not going to hurt her again."

Edward looked between us, his eyebrows raised. "Yours? Interesting. Regina never struck me as the kind of woman who'd be into... that."

I bristled, my hands clenching into fists. But Harley's hand on my arm tightened, grounding me, reminding me to stay calm. "What Regina is or isn't into is none of *your* concern," I said. "Now, I suggest you leave before we make you leave."

Edward eyed at us for a long moment, then shrugged, a smug smile on his lips. "Fine. I'll go. But I'll be back. Regina and I have things to discuss. And I won't let the two of you get in the way of that."

He walked away, leaving Harley and me standing in the doorway, fury and disbelief coursing through our veins.

"What the fuck is he doing here?" I growled, turning to look at Harley.

Harley shook his head, his expression grim. "I don't know. But we need to warn Regina. She needs to know he's here."

I agreed, determination settling in my gut. "Let's finish dinner. We'll tell her when she gets back."

But as we turned back to the kitchen, a sense of unease settled over me. Edward's appearance had thrown a wrench in our plans, a dark cloud hanging over what was supposed to be a happy, joyous occasion.

We worked in silence, the steaks sizzling in the pan, the potatoes boiling on the stove. But the excitement, the nervous anticipation that was there before had vanished, replaced by a heavy, dreadful feeling.

Just as we were setting the table, the front door opened, and Regina walked in. She was dressed in a simple sundress, her hair loose and flowing, her cheeks flushed from the walk. She looked beautiful, radiant, and my heart acheed at the thought of what we had to tell her.

"Hey, guys," she said, smiling at us. "Something smells amazing."

Harley and I exchanged a glance, and I saw the worry in his eyes. But we had to tell her. We could't keep this from her.

"Regina," I started, my voice gentle. "There's something we need to tell you."

Her smile faded, concern replacing the joy in her eyes. "What is it? What's wrong?"

Harley took a deep breath, stepping forward. "Edward was here. He came to the cabin. He wants to talk to you."

Regina's face paled, her eyes widening in shock. "Edward? Here? How... how did he find me?"

I shook my head, anger and frustration boiling inside me. "We don't know. But he said he'll be back."

Regina glanced between us, her expression a mix of disbelief and fear. "I... I can't believe he's here," she whispered. "What does he want?"

Harley stepped closer, his voice soft and soothing. "We don't know, baby. But whatever it is, we're here for you. We won't let him hurt you again."

Regina looked up at him, her eyes filled with gratitude and love. "I know," she said. "I know you won't."

She rattled in a deep breath, her shoulders squaring with determination. "Let's eat. We'll deal with Edward later. Tonight, I just want to be with the two of you."

Pride and love swelled in my chest. That's our girl. Strong, brave, resilient. No matter what happened, no matter what Edward wanted, we would face it together. The three of us. As it should be.

Dinner passed in a blur, the conversation forced and stilted. Regina picked at her food, her appetite clearly gone. Harley and I tried to keep the conversation light, trying to distract her from the dark cloud hanging over us. But it was no use. The specter of Edward loomed large, casting a shadow over everything.

After dinner, we cleared the table, the dishes clattering loudly in the heavy silence. Regina excused herself, disappearing into the bedroom, the door clicking shut behind her.

Harley and I exchanged a glance, the worry and concern reflected in our eyes. "We should go talk to her," Harley said, his voice low.

I agreed. "Let's go."

We made our way to the bedroom, knocking softly on the door. "Regina?" I called, my voice gentle, "can we come in?"

There was a moment of silence, then a soft, "Yes."

We opened the door, stepping into the dimly lit room. Regina sat on the bed, her knees drawn up to her chest, her arms wrapped around them. She looked up at us, her eyes filled with tears, her expression a mix of pain and fear.

"Hey," Harley said, his voice soft and soothing. He sat on the bed beside her, wrapping an arm around her shoulders. "It's all right, baby. We're here."

I settled on her other side, taking her hand in mine. "We're not going to let him hurt you, Regina," I said, my voice firm and determined. "We won't let him anywhere near you."

"I know," she said. "I know you won't. But... but I'm scared.

I'm scared of what he wants, of what he's going to say. I'm scared of... of feeling that pain again."

Harley pressed a kiss to her temple, his voice a low murmur. "You don't have to face him alone, baby. We're here. We'll be with you every step of the way."

I squeezed her hand, my voice steady and sure. "We're not going to let anyone hurt you. Not again. Not ever."

Regina looked at us, her eyes filled with tears, her expression soft and vulnerable. "I'm not going back to him."

"Then don't speak to him. You owe him nothing," Jackson said.

"But I want closure. I want to tell him to go fuck himself. I need to tell him, he'll never hurt me again. I need to tell him I never want to see him again."

We sat there for a long time, our arms wrapped around each other, our hearts beating in sync. The room was filled with a sense of peace, comfort, of certainty. And slowly, surely, the fear and worry began to fade, replaced by a sense of resolve.

But there was a part of me that couldn't shake the feeling of unease. The feeling that this was just the calm before the storm. The feeling that our bond, our happiness was about to be tested in ways we never imagined.

And as I held Regina close, her body warm and soft against mine, I made a silent vow. A vow to protect her, to cherish her, to love her with every fiber of my being. A vow to never let her go, never to let her down, to never let her heart break again.

Because she was mine, she was ours. And we'd do whatever it took to keep her safe, to keep her happy, to keep her heart whole and healed.

No matter what happened. No matter what Edward wanted. No matter what the future held.

And with that vow, that promise, that determination burning in my heart, I held Regina close, my love for her a fiery, unbreakable force. A force that would see us through whatever came our way. A force that would keep us strong, keep us united, keep us whole.

Together. Always. Forever.

The doorbell rang, and we all gazed at one another. The asshole had returned.

CHAPTER 12

The doorbell's echo lingered in the air, a jarring intrusion into the warmth and safety of our secluded cabin. I glanced at Jackson and Harley, both watching me with unwavering protectiveness.

But this was something I needed to do alone. I owed it to myself to end things with Edward without either of them hovering, and maybe—if I'm being honest—I needed to close this chapter without anyone else there to see my humiliation.

"I need to talk to him alone," I said, steeling myself against the storm inside me.

Jackson's jaw tightened. "Regina, you don't have to—"

"Please, Jackson," I cut him off gently, resting a hand on his cheek. "I need to do this. Just give me a few minutes."

"I don't like it," he muttered, his voice low and reluctant.

"I know." I gave him a quick, reassuring kiss, then turn to Harley, whose worry mirrored Jackson's. "Thank you. I'll be okay."

"Just say the word," Harley said, his voice rough, "and we'll throw him out on his ass."

I flashed them a grateful smile, my heart buoyed by their support, even if I was leaving it behind for the moment. I made my way to the front door, each step weighted with the memory of what Edward put me through.

As I open the door, I was struck by how little he's changed. Edward stood there, dressed to perfection, his gaze steady but distant. It was the same look that once captivated me but now felt hollow, a mask hiding his indifference or maybe a hint of regret. But I couldn't allow myself to think that way.

"Regina," he said smoothly, his tone exactly as I remembered it. "You look beautiful."

I crossed my arms, keeping a cold distance between us. "What do you want, Edward?"

He sighed, that all-too-familiar look of controlled weariness crossing his face. "I came to apologize. To explain everything."

"Apologize?" I repeated, my voice thick with disbelief. I stepped outside, grabbed his arm, and dragged him away from the door. I was so mad, I stood toe-to-toe with him. "You left me at the altar, Edward. You humiliated me in front of everyone we knew, shattered my trust, and now you want to apologize?"

He looked down, then back up with an earnestness I barely recognize. "I know. And I can't make excuses, but... I was scared. Overwhelmed. I thought I wasn't ready for commitment, but I was wrong, Regina. I can't stop thinking about you, and I need you to understand that leaving was a mistake. I made a terrible, stupid mistake."

His words almost sounded genuine, but I'd been here before. I let myself fall for his promises once, and it nearly broke me.

"You've made your point," I said coldly. "But you have no

idea what you put me through. Do you even realize what it felt like to be standing in that church, realizing you'd run? You left me with nothing but broken promises."

His expression faltered. "I know. I'll never forgive myself for what I did. I was weak—too weak to see how perfect you are for me."

I shook my head, forcing myself not to waver. "Weak? No, Edward. You weren't weak. You were selfish. You let your family's prejudices cloud everything between us, and then you left me to face it alone."

He turned away, his jaw tense. "My family… Regina, they were a big part of why I panicked. They always made me question everything about us. But now, none of that matters. I'm here, and I'm asking you—begging you—for a second chance."

The desperation in his voice caught me off guard, but it wasn't enough to sway me. "Why? So you can turn around and leave again when they disapprove? I can't go through that again, Edward."

He stepped closer, his hand reaching out as if he might touch my arm. "I was wrong, and I'm asking you to forgive me. Because I can't stop thinking about you. Every single day, I regret what I did more and more. You're everything I ever wanted. You're the woman I want to grow old with, to have a family with."

Disgust rolled through me. I turned to stomp away, ready to never see this guy again.

"Regina, please," he hollered. "I'm still in love with you."

I froze, his words crashing over me. There was a time when hearing him say that would have meant everything. But that time has long since passed. I slowly stepped toward him again, and this time, I got into his face. I'd bite his nose off if he wasn't such a weasel.

"You love me?" I asked, my voice quivering with anger. Behind us, I heard a sound like the door closing. But I ignored it. I had to get rid of this trash before I faced my men again.

He nodded, his hand hovering in the air between us. "More than anything. I know it's hard to believe after what I did, but I'm here, Regina. I'm here to make things right."

"You're here now?" I scoffed. "Where was this when it mattered, Edward? Where were you when I needed you?"

"I was… lost," he admitted, his gaze dropping to the ground. "But I'm not anymore. I know what I want now, and it's you. Just give me a chance to show you I'm the man you deserve."

"The man I deserve?" I laughed bitterly, feeling the sting of his words. "Edward, you're the one who left me. And now you think you can just waltz back into my life because you've decided it's what you want?"

"I know I don't deserve it, but I'm begging you. I'll do anything—"

"Anything?" I asked, fury bubbling up. "Would you stand up to your family? Would you cut them off, once and for all, if they tried to come between us again?"

He faltered, glancing away. "I—"

"That's what I thought," I said coldly. "You don't get it. This isn't about just us anymore, Edward. This is about trust, about loyalty, about love that doesn't just bend when it's inconvenient."

I took a step back, putting even more space between us. "I found that kind of love. Real love, Edward. With two men who actually stand by me, who respect me, who have never once made me feel like I wasn't enough."

His expression twisted, shock and anger mingling together. "*Two* men? Regina, you mean to tell me you're... you're with *two* men?"

"Yes," I said firmly, meeting his eyes without a trace of hesitation. "I'm in a relationship with Jackson and Harley. They're my future. Not you."

He recoiled, his expression darkening. "I can't believe this. I always knew you were different, Regina, but this... this is perverse. You're involved with two men, and you expect me to respect that?"

I laughed, unbothered by his disgust. "I don't expect anything from you, Edward. In fact, I expect you to leave and never come back. Because I deserve better than the love you're offering. I deserve people who actually fight for me, who don't care about anyone else's opinions. And that's exactly what Jackson and Harley give me."

He stared at me, a mixture of betrayal and fury etched across his face. "I thought I knew you. I thought... I thought I loved you. But this... Regina, this is twisted."

I crossed my arms, my decision resolute. "No, Edward. Twisted is leaving someone at the altar because you're afraid of what people will think. Twisted is running back because you can't handle the loneliness. I've found real love. And you're not a part of it."

For a moment, he gawked at me. His face contorted, anger replacing the desperation that was there just moments before. "Fine," he sneered. "You want to throw away everything we had for... for this? I hope you're happy, Regina. But don't come crawling back when you realize you've thrown your life away."

Without waiting for a response, he turned on his heel and stormed off, his silhouette fading into the night. I watched him go, the finality of his departure settling over me like a weight lifting from my shoulders. It was over. Finally, truly over.

I turned back toward the cabin, my heart racing with a mixture of relief and exhilaration. Inside, Jackson and Harley waited, and I knew without a doubt where my future lay.

CHAPTER 13

I couldn't keep still. My feet grinded into the floorboards as I paced back and forth, each step sending a jolt of anger and pain straight through me. It felt like the walls were closing in, trapping me in this sick realization, and I couldn't breathe, couldn't shake the feeling that everything we built was crumbling before my eyes.

I glanced at Harley on the couch. His shoulders were slumped, his face in his hands, his fingers laced so tightly, his knuckles were bone white. He hadn't spoken in what felt like hours, but I knew he was feeling it too—the dread, the disbelief, the rage, and the heartbreak.

We heard every word between Regina and Edward. The apologies. His begging. His talk of second chances. And then he hollered he still loved her and then dead silence. I peeked out the door to see her leaning in to kiss him. My heart dropped.

I slammed the door closed. What the hell just happened? She was taking him back?

I closed my eyes, trying to block out the image of her slowly stepping toward him. Going to him. The thought felt like a knife twisting in my chest.

"She's forgiving him. We can't stay here," I said, my voice rougher than I intended, every word thick with the agony tearing me up inside.

Harley turned to me, his eyes haunted, lost. "Jackson..." His voice trailed off as if he couldn't find the words, and I knew it was because he was hurting just as much as I was. Maybe worse.

I shook my head, unable to look at him, afraid I might break right then and there. "No. We're leaving. Now."

He stared at me, his face a mix of resignation and defeat. "If that's what you want, brother."

I turned, storming into the bedroom and yanking my duffel bag from the closet. I tossed my clothes inside without caring if they were folded or even packed right. I just needed to get out, away from this place, away from her and the painful memories that were suffocating me.

Harley was packing too, but his movements were slow, almost mechanical. I saw the same pain in him that was tearing me up, the betrayal twisting like a thorn in my chest.

When I finally zipped my bag, I took a deep breath, willing myself to go. But I couldn't leave—not yet. A sick part of me needed to hear it from her, to look her in the eyes and know, beyond any doubt, that she'd chosen him. Maybe then, I could walk out for good. Maybe then, I'd finally stop feeling like I was ripping myself in two.

Harley followed as I headed back to the living room, and there she was—standing by the window, her arms wrapped around herself, staring out like she was a million miles away.

She turned, her eyes widening as they land on the bags slung over our shoulders.

"What's going on?" she whispered, her voice tinged with confusion and—hell—hurt. Like she was the one who'd been blindsided. I forced myself to harden.

"We're leaving," I said, my voice cold, flat. I saw the hurt flicker across her face, felt a sick satisfaction watching her flinch. But it didn't ease the hollow ache in my chest, didn't make it any easier to look at her.

"But... why?" She sounded lost, almost desperate, and for a second, I wanted to cross the room, to pull her close, to make her choose us. But I shoved that urge down.

"Why?" I echoed, my voice dripping with bitterness. "Are you serious, Regina? We heard everything. Every word. Every sickening promise and apology he made. And we saw you go to him."

She took a step back, shock widening her eyes. "You... heard? You think you know what you saw?"

"Don't play dumb," I bit out, the anger bubbling over. "We heard enough. Enough to know you're ready to let him back in. That he's got his claws in you all over again, and that we're just... temporary."

She shook her head, her eyes pleading. "You're wrong, Jackson. You're so wrong. Whatever you think you heard, it's not the truth."

My anger flared hotter, and I felt the words tumbling out before I can stop them. "So, what? We're just supposed to believe you? After you let him spill his heart out to you? After you gave him the chance to tell you how much he still loves you?"

She stepped closer, her face flushed with pain, with

desperation. "Yes! Yes, you're supposed to believe me. Because I love you. Both of you. I chose you, not him."

The words hit me hard, burrowing under my skin, stirring something deep, something that almost made me give in. Almost.

"Stop it, Regina," I said, my voice colder than I've ever heard it. "Don't make it worse by lying. We heard you, and we know what we saw. You chose him, and we're not sticking around to watch you tear us apart."

Tears brimmed in her eyes. "No, Jackson, you're wrong. You're both so wrong. I didn't choose him. I chose you. I told him good-bye. I told him it was over."

The pleading in her voice almost broke me, almost cracked through the wall I was trying so damn hard to keep up. But the memory of her kissing him filled my mind, and I just couldn't do it. I couldn't open myself up to be hurt again.

"Enough, Regina," I said, forcing every word out with a steel edge. "We're done here. I can't be with someone who doesn't know what she wants, who's still hung up on the man who left her at the altar. We won't let you drag us down with you. Good-bye, Regina." My voice was empty, final, as I brushed past her, feeling Harley's hand on my shoulder, grounding me, keeping me from falling apart right there in front of her.

As we walked out of the cabin, I forced myself not to look back, not to think about what we were leaving behind. But when we reached the truck, I caught one last glimpse of her standing in the doorway, her body wracked with sobs, her face crumpling as she realized this was real.

And as I pulled away, the pain twisting in my chest told me I was making the worst mistake of my life. That I'd just walked away from the one person who made me feel whole, the future I'd dreamed of. But it was too late. The damage was done. The words were out. The hearts were shattered, and there was no going back.

All that was left was the road in front of us, stretching into a hollow, endless unknown, and the bitter taste of what could have been.

CHAPTER 14

The truck's engine rumbled beneath us, cutting through the night quietness like an unspoken warning. I felt Jackson's tension beside me, his grip white-knuckled on the steering wheel, his jaw tight.

He was wrestling with thoughts of Regina—of what might be happening with that snake Edward who'd come sniffing around, wanting her back. I knew the fear gnawing at him, the hurt.

"Hey, you good?" I kept my tone low, careful.

He took a shaky breath, raking a hand through his hair. "I don't know, Harley. I heard them. I heard him telling her he still loves her, that he wants another chance. And I lost it. The thought of her—going back to him, after everything we've been through—it just…" His words broke off in frustration, and he clenched the wheel harder.

"And you think she'd go for that? After all he put her through? After everything we've shared?"

Jackson glanced over, pain etched into every line on his

face. "I don't know what to think, man. I just know I love her, and I can't stand thinking he got her."

Silence stretched between us, broken only by the rumble of the engine and the crunch of gravel under the tires. I needed to ease the storm brewing inside him. I owed him that.

"Remember when we were deployed, when things were at their worst?" I asked, thinking back to those days in hostile territory where our lives depended on each other's strength. "No matter how bad it got, we had each other's backs. We were a family."

A ghost of a smile lifted the corner of his mouth. "Yeah. Always had each other's six."

I nodded. "And we're still that, Jack. We're a family. Families stick together, no matter what." I paused, letting the words sink in before I added, "And right now, we're making a mistake. We need to go back."

His eyes flicked to mine, finally meeting me head-on, the smallest glint of relief and understanding there. "You're right, Harley. We can't run away from this. Not now."

I grinned, feeling our old determination reigniting. "Damn right. We need to go back, tell her everything—fight for her, the way we fought for each other."

He looked away, jaw set as he weighed the decision, and after a moment, he gave a nod. "Let's go back. Let's fight for her."

Just as he swung the truck around, his phone buzzed, cutting through the silence. He glanced down, frowning. "It's Nathan," he said, putting it on speaker. "Nathan, what's up?"

Nathan's voice crackled through, tense and to the point. "Jackson, the eviction notice worked. Your uncle's out, but he's contesting it. He's dragging us to court in two days."

Jackson cursed under his breath, his grip back to a white-knuckle clutch on the wheel. "When exactly?"

"You need to be in Blessing to prep, ASAP. If you don't show, then the courts will side with him and you'll lose everything."

Jackson glanced at me, torn. I could see it, that brutal tug-of-war between wanting to stay and fight for Regina and needing to settle things back in Blessing. He didn't need to say it; I understood.

I clamped a hand on his arm. "We'll handle it, man. Let's get back to Blessing, deal with your uncle, and then we come back for Regina."

He looked at me, his face softening, a silent thank you in his gaze. "You're right, Harley. We've gotta see this through. For us. For her. For the future we want."

He turned his attention back to Nathan on the line. "We're heading to Blessing now. We'll be there soon."

"Good. But be ready, Jackson—your uncle's playing dirty, and he's not backing down."

"He won't win, Nathan." Jackson's voice was cold steel, the kind that wouldn't bend. He hung up, and the truck was silent again, the weight of what we were about to face pressing in on us. Even if we had to leave Regina for a bit, I knew we were doing what had to be done, fighting for our home and future.

I turned to him, giving his shoulder a solid pat. "All right, let's get this done. Then we come back and fight for her too. All of it. The future we're building."

Jackson nodded, his expression a mixture of gratitude and resolve. "For our family, Harley. For us. For her."

The truck roared back onto the highway, lights piercing the growing darkness, pulling us toward Blessing and the fight waiting there. And as we drove, Regina lingered in my thoughts, every image of her bringing a sense of warmth, of promise. This wasn't just about keeping the ranch. It was about the life we were building—one with her at the heart of it.

Jackson and I fell into a steady conversation, strategizing, tossing around ideas for how to handle his uncle, who'd never liked to play fair. With every mile that slipped by, we could feel the weight of the task ahead growing, but there was also that old feeling of brotherhood, of having a comrade by your side, ready for the fight.

But a gnawing unease gripped me, like an itch I couldn't scratch. It was Regina. I hated that we'd left her. It felt wrong, like we'd left part of ourselves behind.

I tried to shake the feeling, reminding myself we'd be back soon enough. But she was in the back of my mind, no matter how much I tried to push the thoughts aside. Leaving her felt like abandoning something precious, something irreplaceable. We hadn't fully told her how much she meant to us, hadn't convinced her beyond doubt that we weren't going anywhere.

As the sun sank, casting an orange and purple glow over the horizon, the last light fading, my heart was back with her, imagining her waiting, maybe wondering if we'd come back. And with every thought of her, my resolve grew stronger.

The truck sped down the darkening road, and though we were heading toward Blessing, my heart was split. I was there to fight for Jackson's home and his family's legacy, but just as much, I was fighting to return to her.

Each mile took us closer to a showdown with his uncle, and Jackson and I kept going over what we needed to say and do to keep his uncle from tearing everything down. And beneath it all was the knowledge that we were fighting for a future Regina was a part of, one she'd shaped just by being in our lives.

But even with that determination, that commitment, the unease lingered. This felt like the calm before a storm, like we were gambling with something fragile. In the darkness around us, there was a clarity in what we wanted, but also an ache for what we'd left behind, even if it was only for now.

With a heavy but determined heart, I settled into the seat, focusing on the road ahead. We had battles to win and promises to keep. And when we returned to her, it would be with the certainty that we'd done everything we could for a life we'd die to protect.

In that quiet, in the weight of the night, I made my own vow. Whatever happened with Jackson's uncle, whatever awaited us in Blessing, we'd finish it and come back stronger. For Regina. For us. For the life we were willing to fight for, even if it meant facing down the hardest battles yet.

We had something worth holding onto, and we weren't letting it go. Together, as friends, as brothers, as a family. And nothing was going to stand in the way of that.

 watch the taillights of Jackson and Harley's truck fade into the darkness, the silence closing in around me like a shroud. The cabin felt too big, too empty—it was quiet like a pressure sinking deep into my bones.

Outside, the wind whispered through the trees, and somewhere, an owl hooted. But even the night's sounds couldn't fill the void left by their departure. My anger flared, hot and sharp, searing through the shock.

They left. Again. Just like before, just like they always did when things got messy. Navy SEALs, trained to stare down the worst, yet the first sign of emotional chaos sent them running. My fists clenched, nails pressing crescents into my palms as I held back the fury clawing its way to the surface.

I turned from the window, pacing across the room, anger building with each step. How could they? How dare they come back, make me believe we could start fresh, that I could trust them? How dare they make me fall in love all over again, only to walk out?

I stopped in front of the fireplace, staring at the dying

embers. Their scent still lingered in the air, mingling with the warmth of the woodsmoke, a haunting echo of last night—their laughter, their touch, the sweetness of believing in them. It was unbearable like salt rubbed into an open wound.

With a hard kick, I sent a log tumbling, sparks dancing up the chimney. "Damn them," I muttered, my voice a ragged whisper, thick with betrayal. "Damn them both."

I stormed into the kitchen, grabbing a glass from the cabinet, and filled it with cold water. I downed it in a single gulp, hoping the chill would douse the fire inside. It didn't. I slammed the glass down on the counter, the sound reverberating through the cabin like an accusation.

I couldn't believe I let myself be fooled again. I couldn't believe I fell for their promises, their words. After everything, after all the years it took to pick up the pieces they left behind, here I am, picking up shards once more. I pressed my hands against the countertop, forcing myself to steady my breathing. They were gone. They'd shown me who they were—again. And I'd learned my lesson. No more fairy tales, no more second chances, no more love conquering all.

The anger ebbed, replaced by a sadness so deep, it almost brought me to my knees. Tears pricked my eyes, but I swallowed hard, forcing them back. I wouldn't cry. Not for them. Not ever again.

Straightening, I squared my shoulders, drawing strength from somewhere within. It was time to let go. Time to move on. Time to finally leave behind the tangled mess of "what ifs" and "maybe one days" and start thinking about what I wanted, what I deserved.

As I stepped back into the living room, my gaze landed on the pile of blankets and pillows from last night. The sight sent a fresh stab of pain through my chest. I gathered up the bedding, tossing it onto the couch with more force than necessary. As I did, something peered out from beneath the cushions—a small, worn notebook. Harley's.

I recognize it immediately, his thoughts and dreams tucked within those pages, the ones he'd carry everywhere, always scribbling down poems or notes. My sensitive soldier, I used to call him, teasing him about it. With a hollow pang, I flipped open the cover and found a poem—about me.

In the quiet of the night, I find my peace in you,

Your laughter is my melody, your touch my sanctuary true.

With every sunrise, with every star that falls,

I know you are the one, the answer to my calls.

In the chaos of the world, you are my steady ground,

With you, my love, my heart has found its home, its sacred sound.

Through every storm, through every test,

Together we stand, together we are blessed.

Tears blurred my vision as I read each line, a bittersweet ache settling in my chest. How could he write this and then leave? How could they say they loved me yet walk away?

With a bitter sigh, I snapped the notebook shut and tossed it onto the coffee table. I wouldn't be swayed by pretty words anymore. I wouldn't let myself get tangled in promises that meant nothing when push comes to shove. Not this time.

I stood there, rooted in the middle of the cabin, emotions swirling—hurt, anger, and finally, a strange calm settled over me, clear and sharp, and I knew what I had to do. I refused to just sit here. I wouldn't be the woman who was left standing while they decided whether they were brave enough to face their own feelings.

Determined, I headed to the bedroom, yanking my suitcase from the closet. I tossed clothes in without care, grabbing essentials and anything that would fit, not bothering to fold. I needed out of here. Away from this cabin, away from the memories. I needed distance. Space to breathe.

Thoughts of the future filled my mind as I packed, and for the first time, I felt a glimmer of something like hope. Maybe this was my moment. Maybe it was finally time to step away from all the shadows of the past and create a life that was just for me.

I zipped up the suitcase, set it by the door, and took a last look around the bedroom. The ache in my chest was heavy, but beneath it, there was also relief. So many memories here, so many dreams spun and unraveled. But they were just memories now, part of a story I no longer wanted to tell myself.

I walked back into the living room, letting my eyes drift over the familiar surroundings one last time. The cozy fireplace, the kitchen where we shared stolen moments, the couch where we'd whispered promises that now felt like lies. Every detail was a reminder of what I thought we had, what I thought we could be. But it was time to let it go.

I grabbed my keys from the hook by the door, pausing with my hand on the knob. This cabin was my refuge, my safe space, but now it was just a reminder of broken dreams. With a final breath, I stepped outside, the cool night air washing over me like a jolt back to reality.

I locked the door behind me, the bolt sliding into place like a period at the end of a sentence. This chapter was over.

The car engine hummed to life beneath me, a steady vibration that somehow felt grounding. I eased onto the road, glancing in the rearview mirror as the cabin faded into the darkness behind me, shrinking with every mile. And with each turn of the wheel, each mile that ticked away, something shifted within me. A sense of purpose filled me, fierce and unyielding. I knew what I wanted, who I was, and what I deserved.

No more being left behind. No more waiting around for someone else to choose me. I was done giving my heart only to have it broken. I knew now that the only person I could count on, truly count on, was me.

The road stretched ahead, winding and endless, and I let my thoughts wander over Jackson and Harley, our brief reunion, the dreams we'd dared to chase, however fleeting. I allowed myself a moment of sadness, a small concession to what might have been. But I wouldn't dwell. I couldn't. My life was waiting, and it wasn't with them.

As dawn's first light crested over the horizon, painting the sky in soft shades of pink and gold, I felt the past sliding away. I wasn't sure what tomorrow held, but I knew it would be mine—truly and fully mine. A fresh start. A new chapter.

With a heart full of determination, I pushed forward into the sunrise, into a life that was finally free of what-ifs and second guesses. Whatever came next, I'd face it on my terms, and for the first time in a long time, that felt like enough.

This was my dawn, my new beginning, and I was ready.

CHAPTER 16

The courthouse was a silent, looming presence, the kind of place where justice felt tangible, pressing down on you. The scent of old wood and leather-bound law books lingered, grounding me in the weight of what was at stake.

Now, after a week of stalling tactics and unnecessary delays from my uncle's attorney, I sat at the plaintiff's table, my heart hammering hard against my ribs as I waited for the judge to enter. Beside me, Nathan sat like a steady anchor. His presence kept me tethered, reminding me that I wasn't alone in this battle.

Across the aisle, my uncle Martin reclined with a smug, almost bored look. He was convinced he'd already won, as if this was nothing more than a formality. His arrogance twisted something in my gut, making me even more determined. Today, he was going to see just how wrong he was.

The bailiff called the court to order, and the judge entered, her robes swishing behind her as she took her seat. She scanned the documents in front of her, her expression stern and assessing. I took a deep breath, steadying myself. This was it.

Martin's lawyer rose, his voice slick and smooth as he presented their case. His words were oily, crafted to twist the truth, painting Martin as a victim, a man of entitlement and legacy denied his rightful land. He spun tales of debts and promises, making it seem like my uncle was betrayed. I watched him work, feeling my anger simmer. But I remind myself: truth always had a way of shining through. Nathan and I came prepared for this performance.

When it was our turn, Nathan stood, his voice calm and unwavering as he laid out our side. He went through each fact with precision, dismantling the lies Martin's lawyer weaved. He spoke of my mother, Sofia, Martin's sister—the rightful owner of our family land. He described the deed, the inheritance, the undeniable truth of it all.

As Nathan presented our evidence, Martin's facade started to crack. I watched his face redden, his smugness fading to an ugly shade of anger. But he kept his mouth shut, knowing his bluster wouldn't do him any favors here.

The judge's gaze sharpened with each point Nathan made, her expression hardening. When he finally finished, the silence in the courtroom was thick, almost vibrating with tension. She looked over her notes, frowning as if every word from Martin's side only solidified the truth in ours. Finally, she looked up, her expression as unyielding as stone.

"Based on the evidence presented," she said, her voice ringing clear through the quiet room, "I find in favor of the plaintiff, Jackson White. The land in question is rightfully his, and Martin White is hereby ordered to vacate the premises immediately."

A massive weight lifted off my shoulders, and I released a

breath I didn't know I was holding. Relief flooded through me, almost dizzying in its intensity. We won. It was over. I glanced at Nathan, who grinned and clapped me on the shoulder, his eyes reflecting the same mix of pride and triumph I felt.

Across the room, Martin looked ready to explode, his face an alarming shade of purple. He glared at me, his eyes filled with a hatred I could almost feel burning across the distance. But he knew better than to fight now. He stood, his fury spilling over in a low growl, and stormed out of the courtroom with his lawyer trailing behind like a whipped dog.

As the room emptied, Nathan and I gather our papers, the victory sinking in slowly, sweetly. We fought back. After Martin's bullying and deceit, we finally took him down.

But as we stepped out into the sunlight, the relief was bittersweet. The empty feeling in my chest returned, and my thoughts turn to Regina. I wished she were here, that I could share this moment with her, could wrap her in my arms and tell her that it was over, that we had a future now. But she wasn't here. Although it had only been a week, she's somewhere else, living her own life away from this mess. Away from us.

The thought was a gut punch, and my chest tightenedd. I missed her so much it was like a physical ache. I missed her laugh, her stubbornness, her fire. I missed the way she could look right through me and made me want to be the kind of man worthy of her love. But I knew she was not coming back, and I couldn't blame her.

Beside me, Nathan cleared his throat, his face turning serious. "Jackson," he said quietly, "Regina's in town. She's been at her parents' home for a couple days now. I thought you might want to know."

I stopped in my tracks, my pulse quickening. She was here? Close? The thought sent a rush of longing through me, a need so intense, it almost floored me. I could see her. I could tell her everything. I could—

"With Edward, of course," I said, liking nothing better than to sink my fists into his cheeks.

Nathan laughed. "Are you kidding me? Her fathers would hurt that man if he came around here again."

"Wait, she didn't take him back?"

"No way," Nathan said. "I think the family was hoping you guys would work things out."

Oh, how I wanted to, but after all I said and not believing in her, I doubted Regina would have anything to do with us again. Not after I'd let my doubts overwhelm me.

"No." I shook my head, forcing the thoughts back down. "I can't. We can't. She deserves better than us, better than this."

Harley, who'd been walking quietly behind me, stepped forward, his eyes blazing. "Better than us?" His voice was low, barely controlled. "Jackson, she loves us. She wants this. She wants us. Why are we doing this to her? Why are we doing this to ourselves?"

I looked at him, the words catching in my throat, my heart pounding with everything I wanted to say and couldn't. "Because we've hurt her too many times, Harley," I said, my voice raw. "We've let her down over and over. We've given her every reason to walk away, and maybe we need to respect that."

Harley's jaw tightened, frustration rolling off him in waves. He wanted to argue, to fight, but he didn't. I knew he felt the same pain, the same guilt, the same love that was tearing me up inside. We were both haunted by our mistakes, by the chances we wasted, by the promises we broke.

Nathan looked between us, his expression unreadable. "You both need to figure this out," he said quietly, his voice heavy. "Because this limbo you're living in—it's no way to live. Either fight for her or let her go, but don't keep dragging her and yourselves through this."

With that, he walked away, leaving Harley and me alone, his words hanging like a challenge in the air around us. For a moment, neither of us spoke, the silence thick and charged.

Finally, Harley broke the silence, his voice low and steady. "I can't do this anymore, Jackson. I can't keep pretending like she's not the best thing that's ever happened to us. I love her. And I know you do too."

I felt the truth of his words settle over me like a weight. I did love her. I always had. But I was terrified of making her go through another round of heartbreak because we couldn't keep it together.

But as I looked at Harley, his face set with determination, I realized that my fear was only holding us back. And maybe it was holding her back too.

"Jackson," Harley said, stepping closer, his voice insistent, "we can't keep letting fear control us. Regina didn't give up on us. She's always been stronger than either of us gave her credit for. She deserves us giving her a real chance, not us walking away when things get tough."

His words reached inside my chest, and for the first time, something cracked through my doubt. He was right. We owed it to her—and to ourselves—to be brave enough to try.

A surge of urgency flooded through me. "We have to go to her," I said, my voice steady with newfound resolve. "We have to tell her everything. No more excuses. No more running. She deserves to know how we feel."

Harley's face lit up with relief, and we shared a look of

understanding. We were in this together, no matter what happened. And for the first time, I felt like we might actually be ready to give her the love she deserved.

"I know I'm wrong, but I want everything to be perfect. Let's go to the ranch house, see what my uncle left us with and then we'll go see Regina."

Harley nodded. "All right, but I'm ready to see her now."

"Me too, but I've got to know what he did to the house first. Because, frankly, I want her to move in with us."

"Now, that I can agree with," Harley said.

CHAPTER 17

I sat at the kitchen table, a cup of tea cooling in front of me as I talked to my mother. The sun streamed in through the window, casting a warm glow over the familiar room, a room filled with memories, with laughter, with love. But today, my heart felt heavy, my mind clouded with doubt and confusion.

"Mom," I said, my voice soft, my gaze fixed on the steam rising from my cup. "I used to question your lifestyle, you know. Growing up, it wasn't always easy having two fathers. I'd go to my friends' houses, and there would be just one dad. It made me feel different, like we were weird or something."

My mother looked at me, her eyes filled with understanding and a hint of sadness. "I know, sweetheart," she said, her voice gentle. "We knew it wouldn't be easy for you. But we also knew that this was the life that made us happy, that made us complete. And we hoped that one day, you'd understand that."

I looked up at her, my eyes filled with tears. "I thought I did," I said, my voice shaking. "I thought I understood. I thought I accepted it. But then, when it came time for me to make my own choices, I chose differently. I chose Edward because he was safe, because he was normal, because he offered me the life I thought I wanted."

My mother reached across the table, taking my hand in hers, her grip warm and comforting. "And how did that work out for you, sweetheart?" she asked, her voice soft but firm.

I let out a bitter laugh, a tear slipping down my cheek. "Not well," I admitted. "Not well at all. He left me, Mom. He left me at the altar. He humiliated me, he broke my heart, he shattered my dreams."

My mother squeezed my hand, her eyes filled with sympathy and love. "I'm so sorry, Regina," she said, her voice filled with emotion. "I'm so sorry that you had to go through that. But maybe it was for the best. Maybe it was a wake-up call, a chance for you to realize what you truly want, what you truly need."

I glanced at her, my heart aching with the truth of her words. Because I knew what I wanted. I knew what I needed. I wanted Harley and Jackson. I needed Harley and Jackson. They were the ones who made me feel alive, who made me feel whole, who made me feel complete.

"They left, Mom," I said, my voice raw with emotion. "They left me. They didn't even give me a chance to explain. They just assumed the worst and ran. How can I trust them not to do that again? How can I trust them with my heart, with my life, with my future?"

My mother's eyes were filled with wisdom and understanding. "Regina," she said, her voice steady and sure. "Marrying your fathers was the best decision I ever made. It wasn't always easy, and there were times when I doubted, when I questioned, when I feared. But in the end, it was worth it.

Because they make me happy. Because they complete me. Because they love me truly and deeply and unconditionally."

She paused, her gaze intense, her voice filled with conviction. "And that's what I want for you, sweetheart. I want you to find the love that makes you happy, that completes you, that fulfills you. I want you to find the love that makes you feel alive, that makes you feel whole, that makes you feel like you can conquer the world."

My heart pounded in my chest, my mind racing with thoughts, with fears, with hopes, with dreams. Because I knew that love. I've felt that love. I've lived that love. With Harley and Jackson. They were the ones who make me feel that way. They were the ones who made me feel alive, who made me feel whole, who made me feel like I could conquer the world.

But they left. They ran. They abandoned me. And I didn't know if I could trust them not to do it again. I didn't know if I could risk my heart, my life, my future on them. I didn't know if I could take that chance.

My mother saw the doubt in my eyes, the fear, the uncertainty. And she understood. She knew me too well, knew the demons that haunted me, the scars that marked me, the fears that held me back.

"Regina," she said, her voice gentle but firm, "love is always a risk. It's always a chance. It's always a leap of faith. But it's also the most powerful force in the world. It's the force that drives us, that sustains us, that fulfills us. It's the force that makes life worth living."

She paused, her gaze steady. "And sometimes, sweetheart, you have to take that risk, that chance, that leap of faith. Sometimes, you have to put your heart on the line, to open yourself up, to make yourself vulnerable. Sometimes, you have to fight for the love you want, the love you need, the love you deserve. Especially if those you love are two idiots who can deal with the enemy on the battlefield but not their own emotions."

My heart ached with the truth of her words. Because I knew she was right. I knew love was a risk, a chance, a leap of faith. But I also knew that it was worth it. I knew that it was the force that made life worth living. I knew that it was the force that drove us, that sustained us, that fulfilled us.

And I knew I had to take that risk, that chance, that leap of faith. I had to put my heart on the line, to open myself up, to make myself vulnerable. I had to fight for the love that I wanted, the love that I needed, the love that I deserved.

But even as I acknowledge the truth of her words, I couldn't help but feel a sense of trepidation, of uncertainty, of fear. Because what if they hurt me again? What if they leave me again? What if they break my heart again?

The thought sent a wave of panic crashing over me, a desperate need to protect myself, to shield myself, to guard my heart. But I couldn't live like that. I couldn't live in fear, in doubt, in uncertainty. I couldn't live with the constant question of "what if." I couldn't live with the regret of not trying, of not fighting, of not taking that chance.

And so, with a deep breath, I made my decision.

I look up at my mother, my eyes filled with determination and resolve. "You're right, Mom," I said, my voice firm. "I have to fight for them. I have to fight for us. I have to fight for the future we all deserve."

My mother smiled at me, her eyes shining with pride and love. "That's my girl," she said, her voice filled with emotion. "That's the spirit. That's the fire. That's the love that makes life worth living."

With a sense of purpose and resolve, I stood, my heart

pounding in my chest, my mind filled with thoughts of them, with hopes for the future, with dreams of what could be. This won't be easy. There would be challenges, obstacles, setbacks. There would be times when I doubted, when I questioned, when I feared.

But this was worth it. They were worth it. *We* were worth it. The future that we could have together was worth fighting for.

Mom sat back in her chair, a small smirk on her face. "Nathan called about an hour ago to talk to your dads."

She had my attention. Nathan Alley was working on Jackson's case against his uncle.

"Really," I said. "Did they win?"

"As a matter of fact, they did. The boys were going to the ranch for the first time in years. I'm sure Jackson wants to spend the rest of his life there with his own family. It's just a shame he and Harley hadn't found a woman smart enough or tough enough to pull their heads out of their asses."

With a deep breath, I stepped out of the kitchen, out of the house, out into the world. I stepped out with a sense of purpose, with a sense of resolve, with a sense of determination. I stepped out with my heart on the line, with my soul laid bare, with my future in my hands.

I step out, ready to fight for Harley and Jackson.

I stepped out, ready to fight for us.

I stepped out, ready to fight for the future that we all wanted.

As I drove to their ranch a few miles out of town, I couldn't help but feel a sense of nervousness, of excitement, of fear. Because this was it. This was my last chance. This was my final fight. This was my one shot at redemption, at forgiveness, at love.

And after I pulled up to their house, after I step out of the car, after I walk to their door, I knew I had to give it my all. I have to lay it all on the line. I had to bare my soul, to open my heart, to put it all out there.

And I had to make it count.

I knocked on the door, my heart pounding in my chest, my breath coming in quick, shallow gasps. I waited, the seconds ticking away like hours, like days, like eternities. And then, finally, the door opened.

And there they are. Harley and Jackson. The loves of my life. The men of my dreams. The future I wanted, that I needed, that I deserved.

They look at me, their eyes filled with surprise, shock, and disbelief. And I looked at them, my heart filled with love, hope, and determination.

"Regina," Harley said, his voice soft, his eyes searching mine. "What are you doing here?"

I took a deep breath, steeling myself for what was to come. "I'm here to fight for you," I said, my voice firm. "I'm here to fight for us. I'm here to fight for the future that we all deserve."

They stared at me, their eyes filled with emotion, with love, with hope. And I knew that this was it. This was the moment. This was the chance. This was the fight.

And I was ready.

And I was going to win.

CHAPTER 18

I opened the door, and there she was—Regina, standing on our doorstep, her eyes bright with determination. My heart was hammering, and I could feel Jackson tense beside me. This was what we wanted, what we both dreamed of, but right now, it felt like a second chance we might not deserve.

"Regina," I said, my voice barely a whisper, a mix of disbelief and relief all at once. "You have no idea how much we wanted to hear those words."

She met my gaze, steady and unyielding. "I mean it, Harley. I mean it, Jackson." Her eyes flicked between us, and there was a strength there, a fire that was both familiar and new. "I'm here to fight for us. I'm here to make this work. I'm here to tell you that Edward is no longer in the picture at all. Never was and never will be."

"I'm glad," I said as I stared at her thinking I'd never seen her more beautiful.

"I thought you were taking him back," Jackson said.

She shook her head. "Never. You were wrong. It's the two

of you I want more than anything."

Jackson stepped forward, swallowing hard, his expression serious. "We want that too. But we have to talk. We need to be honest about what we want and what we're afraid of." His voice was steady, but I saw his hands clenched by his sides, the way he was fighting his own nerves.

She nodded and stepped inside as we closed the door behind her. The silence stretched between us, thick with all the words we'd held back, the fears we hadn't dared speak out loud. I led her to the living room where there was a ragged recliner and two chairs with threadbare material.

"Sorry about the whole place" Jackson said, looking around. "My uncle really did a number on the beautiful house my mother had." If we was lucky, we'd have a new woman to remake this into a home.

"I'm not worried about that," she said. "I am worried why you didn't trust me."

I felt the weight of those words.

"You're right," Jackson said. "I was wrong."

"You were," she said.

The air was tense and yet I knew in my heart we were working things out. We needed to resolve all of our differences and there was one I'd felt guilty about for years.

"Regina," I began, trying to find the words, "we need to talk about why we left. The first time. Why we joined the Navy."

Her eyes soften as she looked at me, a mix of pain and understanding there. "I know why you left," she said quietly. "You were young, looking for adventure, wanting to serve. I get that. But it still felt like you were running—from me, from us. Like we were just part of something you wanted to escape."

Jackson leaned forward, his elbows on his knees, his gaze fixed on her. "We weren't running from you, Regina. We were running to something. We thought we needed some sense of purpose. We thought we had all the time in the world, that we could have both the adventure and come back to you."

I nodded, the regret heavy in my chest. "But we were wrong. We learned that too late. Being with you—it was the one thing that felt like home, like something real. And leaving it behind was the hardest damn thing we ever did."

She looked down, her fingers lacing together. "So if I was what you wanted, what you both wanted, then why did you leave again?" She glanced up, her voice catching. "Why did you run the second you thought I might be getting back with Edward?"

I ran a hand through my hair, fighting the frustration still as sharp as it was that night we left. "Because we were scared, Regina. We were afraid we were just a rebound for you, a way to fill the void. We worried you'd go back to him, that you'd choose the safety and stability he offered over us. Over... everything we wanted to build with you."

Jackson's expression was pained. "We've never been great at opening up, at being vulnerable, at taking those kinds of chances. We ran because we thought it'd protect us. And that's on us. We're cowards."

Regina reached out, taking both our hands, her grip warm and grounding. Her voice was soft but filled with conviction. "You're not cowards," she said gently. "You're human. You made a mistake, and so did I. I should've been clearer, should've fought harder to keep you here. I should've made you see that I didn't want anyone but you. But I'm here now, and I'm not letting you go."

Her words wrapped around me, each one sinking deep, erasing layers of doubt. I felt the dread lift, replaced with something steadier, more certain.

"Regina," I said, squeezing her hand, "we want this to work more than anything. But we need to know that you're sure. That we're not just…your way of moving past what happened with Edward." I paused, my throat tight. "We need to know this is what you want."

Her gaze held mine, unwavering. "I am sure," she said, her voice steady. "I've spent too much time letting fear stop me from saying it, but I love you, Harley. And I love you, Jackson. I want this. I want a life with you, both of you. I want the kind of love that's worth fighting for. And I don't want to waste another second pretending I don't."

Jackson's hand covered hers, his thumb brushing across her knuckles. "And we want that too. We're all in, Regina. But…we can't endure the pain of leaving you or you leaving us again. We need to know this is for real, for all of us."

She reached up, cupping his face, then mine, her touch soft but grounding. "It is real. This is where I want to be, with you, with both of you, and I'm done holding back. I know what I want, and I want you, for the long haul. No more running."

A wave of relief flooded through me, and it was like the ground beneath my feet finally was steady. But there was a flicker of fear still lingering, a voice in the back of my mind whispering that this might be too good to be true. What if it didn't last? What if we ended up right back here, broken all over again?

She seemed to sense my hesitation, her gaze shifting between us, filled with love and determination. "I know you're both scared. I am too. But I need you to trust me—to believe in what we have here. Because I do. I believe in us, in our future, in the love we share. And I need you to believe too."

The conviction in her voice hit me, and the last of my

doubt began to unravel. I could see it in her eyes, the certainty, the love she had for both of us, as if it was the only thing she'd ever known. And it was enough.

I took a deep breath, the words forming in my chest, and when they come, they felt like a promise. "I believe in you, Regina. I believe in us. I believe that what we have here is worth every risk. And I'm done being scared of it."

Jackson nodded, his face breaking into a slow smile. "Same here. I'm ready to fight, Regina. For us. For everything we could be."

Her face softened, and there was a light in her eyes I hadn't seen in so long, one that made my heart race with hope and certainty. "That's all I needed to hear," she whispered, pulling us both into a hug that felt like coming home.

As we held her, I felt the last of my fears disappear, replaced by the steady warmth of her love. We were here, together, where we'd always belonged. And nothing else mattered.

After a long moment, she pulled back slightly, her expression shifting, growing serious. "But there's one thing I need from both of you." Her tone was firm, her gaze unwavering. "If I send you a message, if I reach out—if I need you—you have to be there. No hesitation. No fear. No excuses. Just...*be there*."

Her words hit like a promise we should've made long ago. Because she was right. Love was showing up, no matter the cost, no matter the doubts. It was standing by the other person, through every twist, every challenge.

I held her gaze, my heart swelling with a new resolve. "I promise, Regina," I said, my voice rough but sure. "If you call, I'll be there. No hesitation. No excuses. You can count on it."

Jackson nodded, his hand resting over hers. "Same here. You call, we come. No matter what. That's how it'll be."

A tear slipped down her cheek, and she gave us a smile filled with love and relief. "Thank you. That's all I needed."

And then she leaned in, pressing a soft, lingering kiss to my lips, then Jackson's, each touch a promise, a beginning, a vow. We kissed her back, feeling her warmth, her strength, the love she was giving us, unguarded and complete. In this moment, everything was perfect. Everything felt right.

We stood there in the quiet, arms wrapped around each other, hearts beating as one, futures entwined. I felt the strength of our connection, the weight of our commitment, and I knew this was where I was meant to be.

This was the love we'd fought for, the future we'd been waiting for. And as we held her close, as we let ourselves believe in the future we were building together, I was ready to claim it.

CHAPTER 19

I stood in front of the full-length mirror in my bedroom, my heart pounding in my chest as I gazed at my reflection. The wedding gown I wore was the same one I wore a month ago but with a few alterations that Edward's mother refused me. It was a symbol, a testament to my past, but also a promise of a new beginning. Today, I was taking a chance, a leap of faith, and I was doing it in the most dramatic way possible.

The silk fabric rustled as I moved, the intricate lace detailing catching the light, shimmering softly. My hair was swept up in a loose bun, tendrils framing my face, and my makeup was subtle, accentuating my features without hiding them. I wanted to look like myself, like the woman Jackson and Harley loved, like the woman who was ready to commit to them forever.

I took a deep breath, steadying my nerves as I picked up my phone. My fingers hovered over the screen for a moment before I type out the message that would seal my fate. "Meet me at the church. Wear a suit." I hit *send* before I could second-guess myself, before the fear and doubt crept in and convinced me to back out.

This was it. This was the test. This was the moment that would define our future, that would prove whether Jackson and Harley were truly ready to commit, to be there for me, to fight for us. And I was terrified. Terrified that they wouldn't show up, that they'd leave me standing alone at the altar once again. But I was also hopeful. Hopeful that they'd prove me wrong, that they'd show up and sweep me off my feet, that they'd give me the happily ever after I'd always dreamed of.

I slipped my phone into my clutch and made my way downstairs where my parents waited for me. Their faces were a mix of concern and hope, their eyes reflecting the same fears and doubts swirling in my mind. They'd been by my side through it all, through the heartbreak and the pain, through the tears and the sorrow. And they were here now, supporting me, loving me, hoping for the best but preparing for the worst.

"Regina," my mom says softly, her eyes welling with tears as she took in my appearance. "You look beautiful, sweetheart."

My dads stepped forward, each taking my hands into theirs, the grip strong and steady. "Are you sure about this, Regina? Are you sure you want to go through with this?"

I looked at them, my eyes filled with determination and resolve. "I'm sure," I said firmly to both. "I love them. I love Jackson and Harley. And I want to spend the rest of my life with them. I want to marry them, today, right now. And I need to know they want the same thing. I need to know they're ready to commit, to be there for me, to fight for us."

My mom smiled, her eyes filled with pride and love. "Then let's go," she said. "Let's get to the church and wait for your men. Let's give them the chance to prove themselves, to prove their love for you."

And so, with my parents by my side, I made my way to the church. The same church where I was supposed to marry Edward, the same church where I was left standing alone at the altar. But today, it felt different. Today, it felt like a new beginning, like a chance to rewrite my past, to create a new future.

As we walked down the aisle, I could feel the weight of the memories, the echoes of the past, the whispers of the pain and the heartbreak. But I also felt a sense of hope, of anticipation, of excitement. And I was ready to embrace it, to cherish it, to live it, to love it.

We reached the altar, and my parents took their seats in the front row, their eyes filled with love and support, their hands clasped tightly together. I stood there, alone, my heart pounding in my chest, my mind racing with thoughts, with fears, with hopes, with dreams. And I waited.

Minutes ticked by like hours, each second stretching into eternity, each moment filled with agonizing anticipation. The doubts crept in, the fears whispered in my mind, the memories of the past threatened to overwhelm me. But I pushed them aside, focusing on the present, on the hope, on the love.

Then, suddenly, the doors of the church crashed open, and there they were. Jackson and Harley, stumbling over each other to get inside first, their eyes locked on me, their faces filled with love and determination. They were wearing suits, just like I asked, and they looked breathtakingly handsome, like the heroes of my dreams, like the men I was ready to spend the rest of my life with.

They started down the aisle, their steps sure and steady, their gazes never wavering from mine. And with each step they took, my heart swelled with love, with joy, with relief. Because they were here. They showed up. They proved their love for me, their commitment to us, their willingness to fight for our future.

As they reached the altar, they took their places beside me, their hands reaching out to take mine, their fingers intertwining with mine, their grip strong and steady. And I knew, in that moment, that everything was going to be okay.

The minister began the ceremony, his voice echoing through the church, his words filled with love, promise, and hope. And as we stood there, hand in hand, heart to heart, soul to soul, I knew this was it. This was the moment. This was the chance. This was the future.

This was our happily ever after.

And as we said our vows, as we promised to love and cherish and honor each other, as we slipped the rings onto each other's fingers, as we sealed our love with a kiss, I knew that this is just the beginning. The beginning of a beautiful adventure, a wonderful journey, a lifetime of love and happiness and joy.

I was ready to love them, to love Jackson and Harley, to love us.

Forever.

CHAPTER 20

The sun had long since set, and the last of the wedding guests had finally left. The house was quiet, save for the soft crackling of the fire in the hearth. I couldn't believe we were here, that Regina was finally ours, forever.

The ceremony was simple, just like she wanted, with our families and close friends gathered in the church. Seeing her standing at the altar patiently waiting to see if we would show had made my heart ache. Thank God, Edward had gotten cold feet.

Regina had been a vision, her dress flowing behind her, and the way she looked at us—it was as if the world had fallen away, and it was just the three of us.

Now, as I sat here on the couch, watching the fire cast dancing shadows on the walls, I heard Harley and Regina laughing softly in the kitchen. They were cleaning up the last of the dishes, insisting that I rest. I'd been on edge all day, not from nerves but from anticipation. I knew what tonight meant for all of us. It wasn't just about sex; it was about sealing our bond, about truly becoming one.

I stood, the floorboards creaking softly under my weight, and made my way to the kitchen. Leaning against the doorframe, I watched them for a moment. Harley was at the sink, his sleeves rolled up, and Regina was drying the dishes, her eyes sparkling with happiness. This was what I'd always wanted—this simple, domestic bliss. I cleared my throat, and they both turned to look at me.

"You two done in here?" I asked, a slight grin tugging on the corners of my mouth.

Regina raised an eyebrow, a playful smile on her lips. "Why, Jackson, you looking to make a mess?"

I chuckled, pushing off the doorframe and stepping into the kitchen. "Something like that," I said, taking the dishtowel from her hands and tossing it onto the counter. I pulled her close, her body fitting perfectly against mine. Harley turned off the tap and dries his hands, his eyes never leaving us.

"I think it's time we take this party elsewhere," he said, his voice low and husky.

Regina looked up at me, her eyes filled with desire and something more—trust, love. I leaned down and captured her lips in a slow, deep kiss. Her body melted into mine, and I could feel her heart racing, matching my own. When we broke apart, we were both breathless. I glanced at Harley, and he nodded, a silent understanding passing between us.

We led Regina to the bedroom, the room filled with soft, flickering candlelight. She stood at the foot of the bed, looking at us with a mixture of anticipation and nervousness. I reached out, cupping her cheek in my hand.

"You okay, sweetheart?" I asked softly.

She nodded, leaning into my touch. "I'm perfect," she whispered.

Harley stepped behind her, his hands resting on her shoulders. "You are," he murmured, pressing a kiss to her neck. She let out a soft sigh, her eyes fluttering closed.

I started to undress her, slowly, reverently. Each piece of clothing that fell away revealed more of her smooth, soft skin. Harley helped, his touch gentle and loving. When she was finally standing before us, naked and vulnerable, I couldn't help but stare. She was so damn beautiful, and she was ours.

Regina reached out, her hands trembling slightly as she unbuttoned my shirt. I let her undress me, enjoying the feel of her hands on my body. Harley did the same, and soon, we were all bare and open to each other.

I pulled Regina into my arms again, kissing her deeply, passionately. Behind her, Harley ran his hands over her body, cupping her breasts, teasing her nipples. She gasped into my mouth, pressing back against him.

I broke away from the kiss, trailing my lips down her neck, her collarbone, her breasts. I took one nipple into my mouth, sucking and licking until she was writhing between us. Harley's hands were on her hips, holding her steady as he grinded against her. I felt her getting wetter, her arousal filling the room.

I looked up at her, our eyes meeting. "Lie down, sweetheart," I whispered. She did as I asked, crawling onto the bed and lying on her back. Harley and I followed, our bodies framing hers. I kneeled between her legs, spreading them wide, opening her to me. I ran my fingers through her folds, feeling her wetness, her heat. She moaned softly, her hips lifting off the bed.

I leaned down, my breath hot on her skin. "Is this what you want, Regina?" I asked, my voice barely a whisper.

"Yes," she breathed, her fingers tangling in my hair. "Please, Jackson."

I didn't need to be asked twice. I buried my face in her pussy, licking and sucking, devouring her. She tasted like heaven, sweet and musky, and I couldn't get enough. Harley leaned over her, capturing her mouth in a deep kiss, swallowing her moans. Her body tensed, her muscles clenching as she got closer to the edge. I slid two fingers inside her, curling them, hitting that spot that made her scream.

She came hard, her body convulsing, her juices flooding my mouth. I lapped up every drop, my cock throbbing with need. When she finally came down from her high, she looked at me, her eyes glazed over with lust.

"I want you," she whispered. "Both of you."

I glanced at Harley, and he nodded, understanding. We'd talked about this, about how we wanted to take her together, to claim her completely. I lay on my back, pulling Regina on top of me. She straddled my hips, her wet pussy sliding along my cock. I grabbed her hips, lifting her slightly, positioning myself at her entrance.

"Ride me, sweetheart," I said, my voice rough with desire.

She slide down onto me, taking me deep inside her. We both moaned at the feeling, the connection. She started to move, her hips rolling, her body rising and falling. I reached up, cupping her breasts, teasing her nipples. She leaned forward, her hands on my chest, her hair falling around us like a curtain.

Harley moved behind her, his hands running over her back, her ass. He spread her cheeks, his fingers dipping into her wetness, coating them before moving to her tight hole. She tenses slightly, looking back at him.

"It's okay, baby," he murmured, pressing a kiss to her shoulder. "We've got you."

He started to prepare her, his fingers slowly stretching her, getting her ready. She moaned, her body pressing back against him, her movements on my cock becoming slower, more deliberate. I felt her getting tighter, her body clenching around me.

Harley looked at me, a silent question in his eyes. I nodded, and he positioned himself, his cock pressed against her entrance. He started to push in, slowly, carefully. Regina gasped, her body tensing. I rubbed my hands up and down her back, soothing her.

"Relax, sweetheart," I whispered. "Let him in."

She took a deep breath, her body relaxing slightly. Harley pushed in farther, and I felt him through the thin wall separating us. It was intense, the feeling of him inside her, of her clenching around both of us. Regina let out a low moan, her body shaking.

"Oh God," she breathed. "It's too much."

"You can take us, baby," Harley said, his voice strained. "You're doing so good."

He pushed in more, and suddenly, he was all the way in. We all paused, our breaths coming in ragged gasps. Regina's heart raced, her body trembling.

"You okay?" I asked.

She nodded, a small smile on her lips. "I'm more than okay."

We started to move, slowly at first, finding our rhythm, our bodies in sync, our breaths mingling. Regina's moans filled the room, her body quivering with pleasure.

I was getting closer, my body tensing. But I wanted to make this last, to make it good for her. I reached between us, my fingers finding her clit. She gasped, her body jerking. I rubbed slow circles, feeling her get wetter, her body clenching tighter.

"Jackson," she moaned, her head falling back. "Harley. Oh God."

We moved faster, our bodies slapping together, our breaths coming in ragged gasps. I sensed her getting closer, her body tensing, her muscles clenching. And then she came, her body convulsing, her screams echoing in the room. It was too much, the feeling of her coming around us, and I couldn't hold back any longer. I came hard, my body shaking, my cock pulsing inside her. Harley followed, his body tensing, his groans mingling with ours.

We collapsed onto the bed, our bodies still tangled. Regina lay on top of me, her body limp, her breaths coming in soft pants. Harley was behind her, his arm draped over her waist, his face buried in her neck.

I looked at Harley, a soft smile on my lips. He smiled back, his eyes filled with love and contentment. We did it. We claimed her, fully and completely. She was ours, now and forever.

We lay there for a while, our bodies cooling, our breaths returning to normal. Regina lifted her head, looking down at me with a soft smile.

"That was..." she started, but trailed off, shaking her head.

"Perfect," I finished for her, pressing a kiss to her lips.

She smiled against my mouth, nodding. "Yes," she whispered. "Perfect."

Harley shifted behind her, pressing a kiss to her shoulder. "You doing all right, baby?"

She turned her head to look at him. "I'm more than all right," she said, her voice filled with emotion. "I'm happy. So happy."

We just held each other, enjoying the moment. But eventually, reality called, and we had to get up. We cleaned ourselves up, taking a quick shower together, laughing and joking like we always did. It felt good, this easiness between us. This was what I'd always wanted, what I'd always dreamed of.

When we got back to the bedroom, Regina crawled onto the bed, her body still naked, still glowing. A playful smile was on her lips.

"So, what now?" she asked, her eyebrow raised.

Harley and I exchanged a look, a silent understanding passing between us. We both knew what we want, what we needed. We wanted to take her again, to claim her, to make love to her until the sun came up. But we also knew she was tired; she had been through a lot today. We didn't want to push her too far.

I sat on the bed, pulling her into my arms. "Now, we hold you," I said softly, pressing a kiss to her forehead. "Now, we love you."

She smiled up at me, her eyes filled with warmth and love. "I like the sound of that."

Harley climbed onto the bed behind her, his body spooning hers. As we lay there, I couldn't help but think about everything that had led us to this moment. All the pain, all the heartache, all the struggles. But also, all the love, all the laughter, all the joy. It'd been a long, winding road, but we'd finally made it. We were finally where we were meant to be.

I pressed a kiss to Regina's forehead, my arm tightening around her. She sighed softly, her body melting into mine.

Slowly, she drifted off to sleep, her breaths becoming slow and steady. I looked at Harley, and he smiled.

This was it, I thought to myself. This was what I'd always wanted, what I'd always dreamed of. This was my family, my home, my life. And I wouldn't have it any other way.

And as I drifted off to sleep, my body wrapped around Regina's, my heart filled with love, I knew that this is just the beginning. This was the start of our forever, the start of our happily ever after. And I couldn't wait to see what the future held.

Because with Regina by our side, with our love guiding us, anything was possible. We could face anything, overcome anything, achieve anything. Together, we were unstoppable. Together, we were complete. Together, we were one.

And that's all that mattered. That's all that ever will.

THANK you for reading Come Home to the Bride. This was the last of the Return to Blessing, Texas series. I've enjoyed returning to this small town, but it's time to move on. Turn the page for a sneak peak at a new series I'm writing. Right now, I don't know if I will continue to write menage series, but I might. If I do, I'll be returning to Treasure Falls., Montana. Or I have another dystopian type of series that's nagging at me. Be sure to sign up for my newsletter to learn what I'm up to next.

Please leave a review. They really help authors.

Want to learn about my new releases before anyone else?

Sign up for my New Book Alert and receive a complimentary book. Blindfold Me.

PLEASE LEAVE A REVIEW

Did you enjoy the book? Reviews help authors. I would appreciate you leaving a review at the retailer of your choice.

Follow Lacey Davis on Facebook.

Sign up for my https://laceydavisauthor.com/mailing-list **and receive a free book.**

CAULDRON ACADEMY

*S*eptember

The three headmistresses of Cauldron Academy, the last all female college for young witches, stood on the second-floor balcony overlooking the swarm of women in the mansion-turned-school's theatre below.

Today, the first semester began. Together, they would educate the next generation of strong, independent ladies and set them upon the world.

"Another year," Tamsin said, gazing at the students checking in. Every year, they seemed younger, though these ladies were considered adults.

"Think of the adventure awaiting us," Alizon replied.

Every nine months was a new risk, undertaking teaching young minds the art of magic.

"Think of the trouble brewing inside these young ladies. Eager intellectuals we will entrust the ancient craft to," Alizon continued. Tamsin wasn't too sure about applying the word *intellectuals* quite yet. But most would get there.

The old mansion seemed to groan as the theater room

filled with shrilled laughing voices, crying, and nervous eyes observing everything.

"Who will be the mischief-makers be this year?" Tamsin asked, knowing a certain family always kept things entertaining. The memory of chasing snakes through the halls, of waking up to owls hooting in their rooms, and zoo animals appearing in their classrooms brought a smile to her lips. The Le Deux girls.

Alizon wiped away nonexistent wrinkles from her stern black dress with its high collar. The pearl choker perfected the schoolmarm-from-the-twenties look. Her closet was stuffed with vintage clothing and she frequented antique stores, searching for old styles and fabrics. It wasn't surprising the twenty-year-olds thought of her as loopy.

Jadis, Tamsin thought, blended in with a more traditional look. If anything, she fit into the modern world around them. Not to say the town of Destiny Falls was modern, but it was now open to anyone moving in. *Normals* just didn't seem to stay long though.

Magic was never put on display. But the strange inhabitants soon had the normals putting for-sale signs in their yards and loading up the moving truck to get as far away as they could—with a smile, of course.

"Hmm," Jadis said, nodding to a group of five beautiful young women, all twenty-two years old. Seniors this year, thank the heavens. "I see the school's most popular group of ladies has arrived." She spoke of none other than the Le Deux girls

"Nine more months, and they will all graduate," Alizon sighed in response. "Nine more months of their pranks before we send them out to defy evil."

All three headmistresses shook their heads.

Tamsin studied the young ladies. "They have good hearts but just can't stay out of trouble."

The large gathering room was full with only a few seats available. "Looks like everyone is here. Shall we begin?"

The smell of musk filled the air and the grand warlock from the Federation of Witches appeared in a cloud of mist at their side.

"Good morning, ladies," he said, gazing down at the students mingling about. "Another year about to begin."

"Yes, sir," they all said, Tamsin trying not to let the fear sound in her voice. She knew why he was here. The grand warlock had not visited the academy in the thirty years they had been the headmistresses of the small private college.

"What do we owe the pleasure of your visit?" Alizon asked, the three of their minds gathering on a collective basis. Tamsin instinctively alerted the other headmistresses that something was up.

With one last glance at the students, he turned to the instructors, his golden eyes garnering their attention.

"Every one hundred years, we must choose five of our kind to sacrifice to the Hell project. Be looking for the strongest, most cunning witches to dedicate to this undertaking. Once you decide, they have no choice but to take on this dangerous endeavor or die."

Tamsin hated this and wanted to put an end to it permanently. For over two thousand years, every century this battle occurred. So far, the witches had triumphed every year. The odds were dangerously against them. Now they would choose the next team, and if they picked wrong or the warriors failed, the gates of Hell would be opened to the world.

"Be watching as to which students you think should be the

doomsday warriors. If even one witch backs out, the world as we know it will be no more."

Tamsin glanced down at the young witches. Which ones would they choose to send to their possible deaths?

"Ladies, have a wonderful school year. I'm certain you will choose wisely. I'll return at graduation when you will give me the names. Of course, you are forbidden to ever mention this to anyone. The Hell project is a very well-guarded secret. Imagine if their parents knew what this year could bring their children."

In a swirl of mist, he disappeared.

The words *arrogant warlock* spun in her head as Tamsin watched him evaporate. The task of deciding who would either succeed or be sacrificed was a heavy burden.

After the scent of musk disappeared, the three of them stared at each other. Fear and dread ruling their souls.

"We cannot make a mistake," Tamsin whispered.

"The world is depending on us to defend it from hell?" Jadis whispered back, her hand clutching her shirt over her chest. "That wasn't in the job description I read when signing on."

Alizon stomped her black granny boot. "Was he serious? Why the hell do we have to be the ones who choose the witches for an event they may never return from?"

The weight of their decision descended on Tamsin's heart as she gazed out at the young women. How could she decide who might live and who might die?

"Lives could be lost. Families destroyed."

They stared down at the students again, each lost in their own thoughts.

"Nine months to choose who will save or end the world."

Available Everywhere

136

LOVING MY COWBOYS

Want to Read the Original Blessing, Texas Series? Book 1 is Free!

Lillian Bradley sat astride a large red mare, gazing out at the rolling hills of Texas, counting the cattle for a third time. Someone was stealing her cows.

With a sigh, her eyes roamed across the land she loved. All this acreage, cattle, goats, horses, and even a bunch of chickens, but they were all she had. Lily was alone.

Yellow fever had raced through her family, killing everyone but herself. Alone, she didn't understand how she had survived, but here she was with a large ranch and no one to help her with the many chores and responsibilities.

Some days, it was more than a body could bear, but she refused to give up.

Dust rose in the distance and she watched as a rider rode toward her. As the stranger drew closer, a groan rose in her throat. Jim White of the Big W Ranch, her neighbor, was coming for a visit. Rather an offer.

The man owned the largest spread in this section of Texas and was known for his shady deals, swindling, and even his prostitutes.

Pushing her long blonde curls back, her hand came to rest on the rifle she had become accustomed to being at her side.

He pulled his horse up beside her. "Good morning, Miss Bradley. How are you today?"

She turned and gave him an irritated frown. The wind blew her blonde hair into her face and she brushed it back. "Someone is stealing my cattle."

"I'm sorry to hear that," he said. "You know, a pretty young woman like yourself shouldn't be worrying over lost cattle."

"Maybe not, but yellow fever didn't give me much choice."

Her mare shimmied nervously, her paws dancing, eager to get away.

"Let me buy the ranch from you. Or even better, have you considered my son Matt? You are of marrying age. We could combine our land together into one big family ranch."

Like hell. She would shoot herself before she'd marry his weasel son.

"Thank you, but I'm not selling my family's land. Their deaths will not be in vain. As for marrying your son, no thank you."

It was all she could do to keep from screaming *oh hell no*. Not Matt White, a mean, cussing, tobacco spitting boy who knew his father would always get him out of trouble.

Mr. White's face turned red and his lips pressed into a thin line, but she didn't care. "A young woman should not be running a ranch."

"And yellow fever should not have killed my family." She sighed and turned to him. "For the last six months, I've taken care of this ranch and I plan on continuing. Need to find a new helper since Mr. Garza disappeared."

The man was like family and she was so disappointed he left her when she needed him the most. For nearly fifteen years, the man worked on the ranch and then one day, he just vanished.

"Miss Bradley," Jim said, his voice coaxing and gentle. "I could take the worry off your hands. You would be free to be the young woman you long to be."

It was true that she pined to have a carefree life again. One where all she had to worry about was helping her mother with dinner or the laundry. Where her grandmother baked a cake every week. Her grandfather and she went fishing when the weather permitted. But those days were gone. Stolen from her by a hideous disease.

"I'm so glad you came by, Mr. White. If you know anything about who might be taking my cattle, tell them I'm a fine shot with a rifle and I will not hesitate to kill them. Also, if you see my helper, Mr. Garza, tell him I would like to talk with him about increasing his salary."

Often times, she worried something had happened to Mr. Garza. Because she didn't think he would have left without saying good-bye. At least, she hoped not.

"Will do, Miss Bradley. You think about my offer. I'm willing to give you top dollar for your ranch."

Top dollar, her ass. The man was a known cheat and would not give her anything for the Sweet B Ranch. Over the years, her father had complained how when times got bad, Ole Jim was there to steal the property for little or nothing from the ranchers in dire straits.

"Good day, Mr. White."

It was a clear signal for him to leave. She had an appointment with the banker later today and she needed to be riding into town but would wait until he was out of sight. Though she doubted he would do something, she could see him setting fire to the house to force her to sell.

The man was a vulture of the worst kind. Preying on the weak and, right now, she was in his sights.

What she needed was a husband. Someone to help her with the ranch. To keep rustlers from cutting the fence and stealing her herd. Someone to fill the house with love and laughter. Someone to help her create her own family.

The big house was empty and creaked and moaned at night. Fear had her sleeping on the horsehair couch her mother had been so proud of.

While she managed on her own for six months, it was time for her to fill her bed. Someone to teach her the ways between a man and a woman. Someone to scratch this itch she knew only a man could fulfill. And she wanted someone to love her and the Sweet B.

Today, she'd donned her prettiest dress. This morning she bathed, fixed her hair with the hot iron, and made certain she looked her best.

She knew what she had to do. After she went to the bank, she planned on talking to the preacher about any eligible young men who might be interested in her as a wife.

It was time to go husband hunting. It was time to find herself a man.

Available Everywhere!

Come Home to the Country
Come Home to the Doctor's
Come Home to the Bride
Return to Blessing, Texas Books 1-3
Return to Blessing, Texas Books 4-6

Treasure Falls Brides
Our Fugitive Bride
Our Desperate Bride
Our Wild Bride
Our Dangerous Bride
Our Lucky Bride
Our Christmas Bride
Box Set 1
Box Set 2

**Want to learn about my new releases before anyone else?
Sign up for my New Book Alert and receive a
complimentary book. Blindfold Me.**

Lacey Davis is the *alter ego* of a USA Today, bestselling author who decided to dive headfirst into the world of sexy romance. Why? Because who doesn't love writing about hunky bad boys and fierce, fabulous women who know how to make them beg for more? With these sizzling stories, I'm here to deliver the kind of romance that will leave you reaching for a fan (or an ice bath—your choice).

If you're into bad boys who like to take charge and strong women who aren't afraid to shake things up, then you've come to the right place. These steamy reads will not only get your pulse racing but also have you cheering for these bold women as they tame their wild men—and leave them wanting more. Ready for a little fun? Come on in, the temperature's *just* right.

www.LaceyDavisAuthor.com
The End